W9-BTD-403

BORN WITH
ERIKA AND GIANNI

Text copyright © 2016 by Lorna Schultz Nicholson

Published by Clockwise Press Inc., 201 Taylor Mills Drive
North, Richmond Hill, Ontario, L4C 2T5

All rights reserved. No part of this book may be reproduced
in any manner without the express written consent of the
publisher, except in the case of brief excerpts in critical
reviews and articles. All inquiries should be addressed
to Clockwise Press Inc., 201 Taylor Mills Drive North,
Richmond Hill, Ontario, L4C 2T5

www.clockwisepress.com

christie@clockwisepress.com   solange@clockwisepress.com

10 9 8 7 6 5 4 3 2 1

Library and Archives Canada Cataloguing in Publication

Born With: Erika and Gianni (A One-2-One Book)
ISBN 978-0-99393-517-6 (Paperback)
Data available on file

Design concept by Tanya Montini
Interior design by CommTech Unlimited
Printed in Canada by Webcom

MIX
Paper from
responsible sources
FSC® C004071

WATERLOO PUBLIC LIBRARY
33420013204434

BORN WITH
ERIKA AND GIANNI

A ONE-2-ONE BOOK

Lorna Schultz Nicholson

CLOCKWISE
PRESS

AUTHOR'S NOTE

Best Buddies is a real program that operates in schools, including colleges, all over the world. Students with intellectual disabilities, including young people with autism, pair up with volunteer peer "Buddies." They meet together, one-to-one, at least twice monthly to engage in fun, social interaction. They also participate in group activities. That said, this is a work of fiction. Erika and Gianni and their friends are fictional characters. Their school, families, and all their situations are also fictional. However, I did a tremendous amount of research and met with many families like Erika's and Gianni's so that I could get the story right. But in the end, it is a work of fiction, and fiction is pleasure reading. So please, enjoy!

To my mother, Mary Hellen Schultz
(May 20, 1923 - August 9, 2015).
You inspired me to read and write.
Thanks, Mom. I miss you.

CHAPTER ONE
ERIKA

Holy Moly, was I excited. A boy at my high school says Holy Moly all the time because he likes comic books. I don't know about comic books but I know a lot about musicals. Yup. I do. My older sister, Karina, tells me I'm *ob-sessed* with musicals. Karina likes that word so I say it too. I said, "Holy Moly, I'm excited," because I had to walk across a really big stage to *au-di-tion* for the musical *Grease*.

I was standing behind a curtain in this place called the wings but they're not really wings. Such a *chill* name for a place that is really just a hall. They're not wings. They can't help you fly and they're not fluffy and soft like a Halloween costume.

To me the stage looked like a wide empty hallway, NOT something that should have wings. The microphone on a tall stand looked like a skinny statue in the middle of the stage. *Whew!* I only had to walk to the microphone to sing my song.

Uh oh. Uh oh. Uh oh.

My legs were shaking and the insides of my stomach felt funny, like I was on a bus on a curvy road. I was on a bus once when we were in Mexico and I was six years old. My dad had to hold me in his lap because I was scared we would zoom right off the cliff. *Zoom. Zoom.* Thinking of that still makes my tummy turn upside down.

And thinking of walking across the stage was making the same thing happen. I had what my mom says is an *upset stomach.*

In my first year of high school I didn't like walking down the hallways. No Way José. The first time I stood in the hallway, I felt like I did right then, backstage. I learned to say No Way José from one of my dad's work friends. I don't even know who José is. But I know two ways to say no. No Way José and No Siree. Well, and NO. The first time I stood in my high school hall it was full of people and I didn't like that, not one little bit. Sometimes I would stand and stare and not move. And I said NO when Karina told me to walk. I can walk down the halls now because I'm in my second year of high school, and it's not scary anymore.

And it doesn't make me feel sick.

But I still had an *upset stomach* backstage.

"You're going to do great," said Gianni. He put his hand on my shoulder. Mrs. Beddington, the best teacher at Sir Winston Churchill High School, put me and Gianni together as Best Buddies in September. He's nice too, like really-really nice, and a good singer and an awesome singing teacher. *Awe-some.* I like that word.

Maybe if I say it I won't feel sick?

"Awe-some. Awesome."

So many kids in my high school say *awesome* this and *awesome* that. Oh, and Karina says it too. Gianni helped me learn my song and he's singing too, right after me.

Saying *awesome* two times didn't help. I still didn't feel very good.

"Maybe you should warm up your voice," said Gianni and

he led me out into the hallway. "Listen to me first then you can try." He opened his mouth wide, made a loud sound, then closed his mouth, puckering his lips and making a different sound. I think he sounded funny like a horse and I know what horses sound like because I took riding lessons when I was eight years old and my teacher's name was Trevor McPherson.

"That sounds funny," I said, staring up at him.

"Just try it," said Gianni. "You'll sing better if you warm up your vocal cords."

I opened my mouth, then closed it, then opened it again and the funniest sounds came out.

"That's good," he said.

"Tickles," I said. And it did. It tickled the back of my throat.

"That's okay. It's a good exercise. Remember how I said you had to focus before you auditioned?"

He was being *soooo* serious, and looking at me without a smile on his face, like he did when he was teaching me to sing. I knew I'd better *fo-cus. Fo-cus. Focus.* I like that Gianni treats me like this because I want to be a good singer and sing like Julie Andrews in *The Sound of Music.* She plays Maria. Sometimes people don't think I can be serious or that I can learn things, but I can—I can do lots of things after I'm serious and listen. And focus. *Focus.*

"Now, repeat the sounds that I make." He opened his mouth and sang, "*Laaaa.*" His voice warbled as he sang a high note. Gianni wanted to be Danny Zuko, the coolest guy in *Grease,* and wear a black leather jacket and comb his hair back with gel. If I got a part I would get to wear a poodle skirt. Yeah! And look pretty!

But first I had to audition. *Ohhh.*

I'd never auditioned for anything before. Nope. My stomach still felt as if I was on a ride at Disneyland, like one of the train rides, when it goes down a big hill. *Whoosh.* My hands had a lot of sweat on them too. Yucky, slimy, gross sweat.

Right then, I needed to *focus* and be serious.

I tried to make the same sound as Gianni, but my "*laaaa*" didn't sound quite the same.

"Good job, Erika," said Gianni. "It doesn't matter what you sound like because the goal is to warm up your vocal cords."

So far, in the Best Buddies program, Gianni and I had gone for hot chocolate—I love hot chocolate, especially when it has sprinkles and lots of whipped cream. Yum. We also went to a dance teacher to learn how to waltz for the Best Buddies Halloween dance and we were *awesome.* We waltzed all over the floor—*one*-two-three, *one*-two-three. And once, for a special treat, we went to see a musical at a theatre. I wore my yellow-and-orange dress that day and tights and pretty shoes, not sneakers.

Uh oh. Uh oh. Uh oh. I wished I'd worn my good shoes for my audition and not my clunky sneakers. I should have worn my good shoes. I should have. But I never wear my good shoes to school. *Oh noooo.*

"Erika, you're next," said a boy named Andrew Long. He held a clipboard and had a headset on his head.

"Erika Wheeler." I heard Mr. Warner call my name. Suddenly, my stomach hurt real bad like I wanted to throw up all over the floor and that would be awful cuz I needed to throw up in the toilet. The girls' restroom was far away too.

"That's you, Erika," said Gianni. "Break a leg."

"Break *my leg*?" I looked up at Gianni.

"I don't want you to *really* break a leg," he said. "That's what you're supposed to say when someone goes on stage. It means to do your best."

"Well, *duh*," I said. "I know I need to do my best."

I stared at the long stage. To do my best I had to go on stage. I wasn't sure if I really wanted to *au-di-tion*. The stage looked big and long and scary, like the halls did at school on my first day. I lowered my head and looked at the floor. I wanted my legs to stop shaking.

"You okay, Erika?" I heard Gianni's voice.

"I dunno." I still didn't look up.

"It's okay to feel nervous," he said. "I always get nervous before I have to go on."

I put my hand on my tummy. "I have an *upset stomach*."

He put his hand on my back. "That's okay. It's called nerves. My nerves always make me feel a bit sick too before I go on stage. But, Erika, your nerves help you sing too. You've practised a lot. You can do this."

I kept my head down because I needed to think. I *had* practised a lot and I'd learned all the words and knew them off by heart. And I could walk down the halls at school all by myself.

"Okay," I said. I lifted my head, put my lips together, and nodded. Then I said, "*They're going down.*"

Gianni laughed. "You're right. They're going down all right. Go wow them."

"I'm going to *wow* them," I said. "I need a hug."

He gave me a hug (but just a short one) before he let me go and pointed to the microphone. Then he smiled at me and winked. "You go, girl."

"I'm going to *wow* them," I said out loud to myself.

I walked across the stage towards the microphone. My knees rubbed together as I walked and my legs shook. My feet clunked along the hard wooden floor. I didn't want my knees to shake and I didn't want to hear myself walk. *Clunk. Clunk. Clunk.* Today I had worn sneakers with heavy soles because my mother didn't want me to slip on ice. *Clunk. Clunk. Clunk.* Loud noises often hurt my ears.

Swish. Swish. Swish. My jeans made noises too as they rubbed together.

I finally arrived at the middle of the stage and I stood right in front of a microphone. Below me was a long table where Mr. Warner, the drama teacher, and Miss Clark, the music teacher, sat. I pressed my lips against the microphone.

"Hel-lo." My voice screeched and sounded loud in the auditorium. I put my hands to my ears because I have sensitive hearing. Some of my friends at the Down Syndrome Society wear hearing aids. I can talk and say big words because I took speech classes and I can sing too. I was going to *wow* them.

"Just stand back a bit," said Mr. Warner. "And it won't be so loud."

Gianni had made me practise saying hello and my name. I listened to Mr. Warner and I moved back, one step, before I said, "Hel-lo. My name is Erika Wheeler." My voice sounded everywhere. I looked up at the ceiling then all around the auditorium. It seemed to bounce a little before it disappeared into the walls. How did it do that?

"Hi, Erika," said Mr. Warner.

They all smiled at me and suddenly my legs weren't shaking as much anymore.

"What are you going to sing?" Miss Clark asked.

"'Oh, What a Beautiful Morning.'" My voice screeched again so I backed even farther away from the microphone. "From the musical, *Ok-la-homa*. I like mornings," I said. Now I liked how my voice sounded in the microphone and I wanted to hear it some more. "Only on Saturdays. Cuz I get to stay in PJs and watch TV with my dad and eat Honey Nut Cheer-ios without milk." It was hard to say *Cheerios* but I did good.

They all laughed and sometimes I like it when people laugh, so I held up my thumb. My *upset stomach* seemed to be going away. Yup. It was.

"Are you singing with music, Erika?" Mr. Warner shook his head at me but it was a good shake.

"Yesss," I replied. My mother told me I needed to *fo-cus* on saying yes and not yup. I liked yup better but not right now.

"Go ahead," said Miss Clark.

I had to take a deep breath first. The shaking in my legs started again. And my upset stomach came back. I couldn't just start singing. I was supposed to look over at Andrew when I was ready and nod at him so he could put on my music. Instead of looking at him I blurted out, "I'm lucky. I was born with an extra gene. My sister has to buy hers." This is my favourite joke.

Backstage, I heard kids laughing and all the teachers smiled. I liked how my voice sounded in the microphone and how it moved around the auditorium. I tapped the microphone and it made a popping sound. *Pop. Pop.*

"Okay, Erika." Mr. Warner was still smiling but I could tell by his eyes that he didn't want to hear any more of my jokes. No Siree. No more jokes.

"We need to hear you sing," he said.

I heard Gianni whisper loudly from backstage. "Sing, Erika."

This time, I looked at Andrew and nodded. I had to *focus*. And now that I had walked across the stage and said my joke, I could. Gianni had helped me with my song and I had memorized all the words and I was on the stage and I liked the microphone. I did. When the music started I listened until it hit the spot where I was supposed to start singing. And I did.

Suddenly, my voice spread around the room and I really liked singing in front of a microphone and how the sound went all through the auditorium. I sang and I sang, all the words, because I knew them off by heart. When I stopped singing, all the kids backstage clapped and so did the teachers. I smiled until my cheeks hurt.

Holy Moly, this was fun!

My stomach didn't hurt at all. No Siree!

"I dance too," I said in the microphone. "Like Michael Jackson." I did the moonwalk backwards then I turned and pretended to lower my hat just like Michael Jackson does in his video. I think Michael Jackson is the best singer in the whole world even if he died on June 25th, 2009. He made up the moonwalk and I'm *soooo* good at it.

I heard the laughter again and more clapping and my face kept smiling.

"Thank you, Erika," said Mr. Warner. "That was really good."

"Yes, thank you, Erika," said Miss Clark.

"It's Gianni's turn," I said. When the list had gone up I'd memorized all the names and time slots so I knew when every person was *au-di-tioning* so I could wish everyone good luck.

I looked to my side and saw Gianni. I waved to him and he waved back. Then I turned back to the teachers. "I worked backstage when I was in middle school."

"We appreciate your getting Gianni for us," said Mr. Warner.

"Thank you," I said and curtsied. Gianni had told me to say thank you at the end of my audition but he didn't tell me to curtsy. That was my *brainiac* idea. My sister is a *brainiac* and her friends say that about her. That's how I know the word. It means smart and sometimes I come up with smart things too, like doing a curtsy.

I walked off the stage and Gianni gave me a hug. "You were incredibly, unbelievably, amazingly, awesome!" He smiled so much at me that almost all his teeth showed.

"That was so *CHILL!*" I squealed I was so happy. Then I hugged him. He is super tall and a skinny-minny.

CHAPTER TWO
GIANNI

Backstage buzzed and adrenalin surged through me, giving me the nervous energy I needed, the high that would help me walk across the stage and perform. I jumped a few times to warm up, big basketball jumps, swinging my arms back and forth. Once I felt the blood flowing through me I tried to find somewhere secluded to warm up my vocal cords. Other people, many my friends, were scattered everywhere backstage and in the hallways, also warming up. A good friend of mine, Sonya, (actually, she's my best friend), gave me a casual wave as I walked by.

She pulled one earbud out of her ear. "Hey, Gianni," she said in that smooth, silky voice that reminded me of caramel.

I thought Sonya was by far the nicest, prettiest and most interesting girl at Sir Winston Churchill High in Erieville. I loved everything about her (including her kindness *and* how she dressed); I couldn't ask for a better friend.

"Break a leg," she said, smiling.

"You too."

"When is Erika up?"

"Soon. I told her I'd help her warm up in five."

"She's pretty excited. She sang her song for me today in the hallway. You've been so good for her." Sonya touched my cheek and I wanted to feel some sort of electrical current, I really did.

"And vice versa." I discreetly ducked my head, hoping to disengage us.

Sonya stuck her earbud back in her ear and I moved down the hall to a private spot. I started with the scales, running up and down them. Up and down. Then I worked through the mouth exercises that my singing coach had given me.

Once my voice was warm, I popped my earbuds in my ears and listened to a recording I had made of myself singing "Can't Take My Eyes Off of You" from the *Jersey Boys* musical. I needed to come across snappy but tough. I'd gone through so many songs trying to figure out the best one to showcase my voice and my ability to play the lead role. I wanted this role so badly I'd hardly slept for the past week.

I needed this to prove myself.

After I'd listened to the song twice, I headed to the backstage area to look for Erika. No matter what, the teachers were going to give her a role, dancing and singing in at least one song at the end of the production, but I was beyond thrilled that they were making her audition instead of just *giving* her the role.

When I spotted her standing in the wings, she seemed to be muttering to herself, gulping big breaths of air. Was she nervous? I kind of thought she would be. In the school hallways Erika was a ham, a natural performer, and she loved an audience—but an audition was different.

"You're going to do great," I said, touching her shoulder. She looked up at me, and her bottom lip jutted out. Okay, so she *was* nervous.

"Maybe you should warm up your voice," I said and steered her out into the hallway. If she was going to be in a musical she needed to learn the ropes. "Listen to me first then you can try." I did a vocal warm up.

She just stood there. Wow. In a way, maybe this was good. Her nerves could give her an edge.

"Erika." I put my hand on her shoulder. "You need to focus. Remember how I said you had to focus before you auditioned?"

She stared up at me, tilting her head, listening to my every word. I sang an easy "*laaaa*" for her, at my higher range, and my vibrato echoed against the walls. She opened her mouth as wide as she could and belted out a "*laaaa*" that, honestly, came out like a donkey braying.

We practised a few more before Andrew Long, the musical's stage manager, said, "Erika, you're next."

"Erika Wheeler." Mr. Warner called out.

Erika looked at the floor and didn't move her feet. Not even an inch. Hey, we all get that sick feeling, especially when it's time to go on stage for the first time. It's an unknown. After a little coaxing and a hug, she walked across the stage.

I breathed a sigh of relief and crossed my fingers.

When she got to the microphone she put her lips right against it. *Oh no.* I smacked my forehead. How could I have forgotten to brief her on how to use the mic? Darn it.

She spoke into it and her voice echoed throughout the auditorium and, of course, because of her super-sensitive hearing, she covered her ears.

"Should I put on her music?" asked Andrew.

"Give her a minute. She knows to nod."

"But can she remember?" Andrew muttered.

I turned and gave him a freezing glare. "She remembers more than both of us combined."

I turned back to stare at Erika on stage. Mr. Warner told her to sing. I waited, tapping my feet. *Come on, Erika.* But instead of singing, she told one of her signature jokes, which, surprise, surprise, made everyone laugh, which was okay because it could relax her, but she really did need to sing. I pressed my fingers to my temple and looked at the floor.

I had to do something about this. "Sing, Erika," I whispered loudly.

When she heard me, she turned to look at me, then she nodded at Andrew.

"Start her music," I said.

"I'm on it." He flicked a switch and her music blared through the speakers.

At exactly the right part, she started singing and I couldn't help smiling, grinning actually. There was nothing wrong with her memory and she didn't miss a word. I swear my heart pumped up two sizes, like I was on steroids or something. Seriously, I felt as if my heart was popping out of my skin with every beat.

"She sounds pretty good," said Andrew.

"She sounds amazing!"

"You're next, by the way."

"Thanks." And just like that my heart shrank, my nerves returned, and I was an electrical mess. Okay, yes, it was time for me to think about my audition. In the wings, I snapped my fingers and practised the choreographed hip movements I was putting into the number.

"Looking good."

I turned and saw Richard Temple walking towards me,

or should I say swaggering. The guy had broad shoulders, the nicest athletic butt and thighs, and a head of wavy black hair that hung to the nape of his neck but didn't look too long or scruffy. He hung out in the school weight room with all the other jocks; a place I generally avoided. I did my own workouts at my own "gym," which was basically a mat and a few barbells in my bedroom.

"How's it going?" He flipped his hair out of his eyes and managed to look way cooler doing it than I ever could.

"You up after me?" I asked. I already knew the answer but I was talking to talk.

"Yeah," he replied. "I'm nervous. Do you get nervous? I mean, you're an actual singer."

"Yeah," I said, surprised at his honesty and interest. "Every time."

He thumped my back. "Good to hear. I swear I could puke." Then he looked onto the stage at Erika, who was now talking to the panel.

I stared at his profile: strong chin, full lips, blue eyes, and this smaller, turned-up nose. He was masculine but cute, an intriguing combination. Why was he auditioning? He was Mr. Soccer star and didn't seem remotely interested in musical theatre.

Richard laughed so I moved to stand beside him and that's when I saw Erika doing the moonwalk. Oh crap. I should have told her to leave that gimmick out.

"She's got that one down pat," said Richard, smiling and shaking his head.

"She does at that," I said.

Once she'd finished moonwalking and chatting *some*

more, she turned and called out to me, "Gianni, you're next."
Then she strutted off stage and wrapped me in a huge hug.

"That was so *CHILL!*" she squealed.

It was my turn next, so I let go of Erika and made my way
across the stage to the microphone.

Silence is a funny word with an interesting meaning
because the world we live in is never really silent. Yes, the
auditorium was silent, as in no one was talking, but I could
hear breathing, fans fluttering, and my footsteps echoing, all
white noise. I've never really heard true silence. Ever. If this was
supposed to be silence, I think it was louder than real noise.

When I stood in front of the microphone I spoke my
name and the part I was auditioning for. Miss Clark looked
down. Mr. Warner flinched. And just like that my heart started
pounding. The palms of my hands oozed sweat and became
slimy and gross. Had they slotted me already?

What was I trying to prove anyway? That I was the best
singer in the school? That I could have a future in music? That
I could play the Ultimate Cool Guy?

That I could kiss a girl?

I nodded at Andrew.

The interlude for my music sounded through the speakers
and I made myself forget about everything else. I sang, snapped
my fingers, and performed the dance steps I had choreographed
myself. I lost myself in the song and sang pitch perfect.

When I was done, I heard the polite clapping and the
spoken compliments but deep down I knew they meant nothing.
When the teachers finished talking, giving me their token "great
work" spiel, they stared down at the table *again*. Had they even
watched me?

I walked off stage toward Erika and her big smiling face. My number-one fan.

She held up her hand for a high five and I tapped it back. A big part of me just wanted to ignore everyone, run out of the auditorium and hide, but I couldn't do that to Erika.

"You did good!" Erika said this with such excitement. "You sang like a bird."

I tried, (I really did), but I couldn't muster the energy to smile. Tears pricked behind my eyes. Yes, I cry. Yes, I'm sensitive. I've heard it my entire life. Who cares? It doesn't mean I can't *play* a macho male lead. I can.

I'm a good actor.

A big wave of relief washed over me when Erika's sister, Karina, showed up to take her home. If I started crying around Erika, she would ask me why I was sad and she wouldn't do it discreetly either.

Once Erika had left with her sister, I bolted down the hall towards the back door and the parking lot. I had to get away from the backstage buzz, which was now like a nasty drone in my head, circling around in my skull, unable to get out.

CHAPTER THREE
ERIKA

"I can't wait to hear him sing," whispered my friend Sonya. She stood beside me and her hair smelled like strawberries. Yum. Sonya is my best friend in the whole world because we have lockers beside each other, since I started high school. Sonya auditioned for Sandy and sang "I've Got Confidence" from *The Sound of Music*. She was *awe-some!* And sounded just like Julie Andrews. It's one of my favourite musicals and I laugh every time they fall in the water.

"He's *awe-some*," I said, clapping my hands.

"You did such an amazing job of your song," said Sonya. "I'm proud of you."

I turned and hugged her and she's not quite as tall as Gianni.

When I heard Gianni say his name into the microphone I stopped hugging Sonya and turned to watch Gianni. When he started singing everything became quiet and I think he sang like a real Jersey Boy from the musical, and just like a real *cel-e-brit-y*. That's hard to say.

"Wow," whispered Andrew Long. "Can he sing!"

"He'll be Danny Zuko," I said.

"He doesn't look like Danny," said Andrew.

I frowned at Andrew. "Don't say that. He's my friend."

"I'm just saying." Andrew walked away from me.

"I hope he's Danny too," whispered Sonya.

I patted my heart before I turned and looked up at Sonya. "You like him?" I know all about boys liking girls and girls liking boys because my sister Karina likes Cameron. I've seen my sister kissing Cameron. I want to kiss someone too.

Sonya scrunched up her nose and smiled. "He *is* cute. And, seriously, the nicest guy in the school. So maybe."

"What about Max?" I stared up at Sonya and squinted. Max played football.

Sonya shook her head. "I'm done with jocks."

"What's a *jock*?"

"Someone who likes sports more than his girlfriend." Sonya put her finger to her lips. "Shhh. We have to be quiet."

When Gianni hit his last high note the teachers stayed quiet for a few seconds but everyone backstage clapped. Sonya and I clapped the loudest because he's *my* Best Buddy and she *likes* him.

He walked backstage, and I held up my hand to high five him. He slapped it back but he wasn't smiling so I didn't put my hand down for my go-low trick. My mom told me not to do my go-low trick all the time. Only sometimes when it is *ap-pro-pri-iate*. Instead I said, "You sang like a *cel-e-brit-y*."

"Thanks, Erika." He still didn't smile.

"Good job," said Sonya. She patted his shoulder.

"They didn't even look up from their notes." Gianni shook his head.

His face looked droopy like a sad puppy with no home. Like the ones on TV.

"Don't be sad," I said. Why was he sad? I didn't want to see him sad.

"Erika!" My sister poked her head around the corner. "Are you finished?"

"Yup," I answered. I can say yup when it's just Karina. My sister's name is Karina Wheeler and she is seventeen years old and in grade twelve and she will be eighteen on May 1st. I'm in grade ten and I will turn fifteen on my birthday on March 12th. This year my mother said I could have cupcakes for my birthday but Karina said she doesn't care if she has cupcakes or cake. *What-ever.* Everyone says *what-ever* and Karina says it all the time.

"How'd it go?" she asked me.

"She was fabulous," said Gianni. "She even did the moonwalk."

"Oh no," said Karina. "Seriously?"

I crossed my arms and frowned at her.

"Whatever," said Karina and she rolled her eyes.

"Yup," I said. "*What-ever.*"

"She was amazing" said Sonya, putting her arm around me. "And she's right, Karina. They did like her moonwalk."

"Well, that's good," Karina put her hand on the top of my head. "Come on, girl, let's get home."

"I have to get my coat," I said.

Karina and I walked to my locker. Sometimes, after school, when she wanted to get home in a hurry, she walked faster than me and ahead of me but today she walked right beside me. Sometimes I am a slowpoke.

"I'm proud of you," she said.

"Thank you."

We got to my locker and I opened my lock like I did every day: twice around, then once backward, then halfway forward once. When it opened, I got out my coat and my favourite red-and-brown plaid tam hat. I wear it every day in the winter. I like to wear the same thing.

"Do you have homework?" Karina asked.

I didn't like doing homework.

"You need to take your books if you have homework."

"No Way José. No homework." I took out my backpack, shut my locker, and clicked the lock closed.

"Okay." Karina shrugged. "It's not my job to make you do your homework. Let's get home then. Mom probably has dinner ready and *unlike you,* I have a ton of homework."

All the way home in the car, we listened to the *Grease* CD. Gianni had bought it for me when I told him I wanted to audition instead of working backstage. As soon as I walked in the side door that led into the kitchen, my mother came out to see me, even before I got my coat off. "How was your audition, Erika?"

"It was *CHILL*," I said. I took off my coat and hung it up on a hook that was just for my coat.

"She did the moonwalk," said Karina. She flipped off her shoes.

"I like Michael Jackson." I said that to *uppity* Karina. That's what my mom calls her sometimes. She says, don't get uppity, Karina. I put my backpack on the floor. "'Billie Jean' is my favourite."

"We know," said my mother and Karina at the same time.

"I'm hungry," I said.

"We're having lasagna." My mother turned and walked back into the kitchen.

A tinfoil pan sat on the kitchen counter. My mom worked

in a big office and looked after my father and me and Karina, so sometimes she bought our dinners from the grocery store.

"I'd like you to feed your father, please. Before we eat," said my mother.

Feeding my dad was my job. When I went into the living room, he was sitting in his wheelchair, watching the news, and he was still wearing his pajamas and housecoat. He always watches the news at five o'clock but I don't like watching the news with him. No Siree. So many bad things are on the news. I like watching musicals or Family Channel.

My dad had been in his housecoat every day this week when I got home from school and my mother wouldn't be very happy about that. No Siree again. My mom thinks he should get dressed in clothes every day but I understand my daddy because on Saturdays I *looove* wearing my pajamas all day when I watch Family Channel.

My dad has something called ALS, which means some of his muscles have stopped working. My mom told me that. I don't really get what's wrong with him but that's because I don't want to and I don't listen when my mom or Karina tell me. Instead I put my hands on my ears and shake my head.

Daddy used to sit on a real chair and walk with canes and go to work but now he sits in a wheelchair. During the day he sometimes works on his computer but he has to wear a funny thing on his head because his hands don't work too well. My mom and Karina have to help him get in and out of his wheelchair. He does a lot of exercises with a lady named Shelley and a man named Antonio. Shelley comes in every day and Antonio comes sometimes. Just a few days ago, my dad told me he wanted to eat in the family room instead of at the kitchen table. My mother wanted him to eat at the table but he said NO because he hates how his food has to be mushed up. He didn't say No Way José or No Siree, he just said NO. I want him to eat in the family room too because then it's our special time.

I plopped down on the sofa and sat beside him because his wheelchair was beside the sofa. I curled my legs up and put my cheek on his arm. "I *au-dit-ioned*." I liked this word. "It was my first time and I did it."

"That's good." He speaks slowly but I always understand him. He didn't always talk like this. When I was little, he could talk and sing *awe-some* and we always sang out loud to songs on the radio. I didn't say *awe-some* when I was little because it wasn't a word in my brain yet. Now I sing songs out loud with Gianni but not my dad. Inside my body, my heart really hurts, like it's being pricked with a needle over and over. I hate needles. Yuck. I wished he could still sing "My Favourite Things" from *The Sound of Music*. I liked it when we sang about the ponies. When I was just six years old my dad put me on a pony and we walked around and around and the pony liked me. I fed him a piece of apple and he ate it in one bite. *Chomp. Chomp.* But he wasn't cream coloured. He was brown.

"I will wear a poodle skirt," I said.

"Nice," he said.

"Can you come watch me?"

He reached for my hand. His fingers felt stiff and a little cold like they'd been in the refrigerator. I squeezed them. He squeezed mine back but his squeeze wasn't very hard anymore cuz his thumbs had ALS.

My mother walked in the room with a bowl of lasagna that looked more like orange oatmeal than lasagna. She handed it to me and she also handed me a damp cloth. "Thanks, Erika. When you're finished, your dinner is ready in the kitchen," she said. "Call me if he starts to choke, okay, honey?"

"Okee-dokee," I said.

I scooped some lasagna on a spoon. "Open up." My dad's hands don't work very well and his food has to be mashed up. His throat doesn't work very good either. I know my mom gets scared when he coughs and sometimes she hits his back. I don't like it when that happens and I put my hands over my ears or sometimes I run and hide under my covers.

I put the spoon to his mouth and he opened it, just like a bird would do if someone gave it a worm. I saw a picture of a bird eating a worm in a book that's why I know that he looks like a bird. I fed him one mouthful at a time and when food dribbled on his face, he let me wipe it off. It was my job to make dinner once a week too. I always make the same thing: mac and cheese. Yup, always mac and cheese.

"Look." I tipped the bowl upside down. "You ate it all."

He swallowed but it always took him a long time to get the food down his throat so I waited for him to finish. "Go," he said. "Eat your dinner."

"I smell garlic bread." I rubbed my tummy before I kissed my daddy's cheek and went to the kitchen.

I sniffed the air when I walked into the kitchen. "Smells *awe-some*." I slid into the chair that was my chair. No one else sat in my chair at mealtime. My mother placed a plate of lasagna in front of me and I picked up my fork. "I'm so hungry, I could eat an elephant."

"Where'd you learn that one?" Karina asked.

"In the lunchroom," I said.

After dinner, I took my plate to the counter because I always take my plate to the counter. Then I went to see my father. I'd rather sit with him and not do my homework.

"I'll read to you," I said.

"Good," said my dad, closing his eyes.

I started reading one of my favourite books. It was a *Whatever After* book about a girl like Ariel, the Little Mermaid. I loved that movie and could sing all the songs. My mother always says that when I was little, I sang before I talked. Sometimes I tell people that, like teachers and kids at school. The book had some pictures but it was a chapter book and I was doing *awe-some* with my reading because I could read chapter books. But I still liked the pictures.

"I like reading the same page," I said to Daddy, "cuz I know all the words."

"I know," he said. "Practice makes perfect."

After reading my one page, my dad's head fell forward and I knew he had fallen asleep. I put the book down and leaned against him. I hoped my mother wouldn't come in and tell me to do my homework because I just wanted to sit with my dad and that's why I didn't bring it home.

CHAPTER FOUR
GIANNI

The blue afternoon had turned to a deep mauve dusk, and a pre-winter wind howled. I yanked my pseudo winter jean jacket on as I scanned the huge parking lot. Empty. I breathed a sigh of relief and ran to my car, got in, and locked my door. Mission accomplished. I'd made it safely to my car, and, believe me, that wasn't a guaranteed easy feat these days.

All the way home in the car, I smacked the steering wheel, until the sides of my hands hurt. I pulled into the driveway, pressed the garage door remote, and yelled out loud when I saw that my older brother had scooped the one parking spot that we shared. I closed my eyes. *Calm down, Gianni.* Compared to my audition it was the least of my worries.

When I walked in the back door my mother was in the kitchen. Like a true Italian, she liked to cook, feasts actually. The table was set for seven which meant everyone was home tonight. Along with three siblings (three brothers), my grandmother (we call her Nonna) also lives with us, She took my old room when I got the go-ahead to share the basement with my older brother.

"So, how did it go?" my mother asked. She stirred something in a big pot, her strong arms moving in a very specific rhythm.

"Great!" I had to keep my voice upbeat.

"What was great?" my nonna yelled, pushing her walker along the kitchen floor, almost bumping into the island. She likes to turn her hearing aid down and tune everyone out, but then she'll want to join in the conversation. So she yells a lot.

"I had an audition today," I said, almost yelling too.

"A *what*?" she screeched.

"An audition, Nonna. I tried out for the musical *Grease*."

She waved her hand in front of her face. "Olive oil works better than grease."

The back door slammed and my father walked into the kitchen and put his briefcase down. The guy timed everything just perfectly, and I knew my bad day was close to its peak.

"Gianni had an audition today," Mom said to my father.

"Good for you." He paused. "A young engineer came in today and was he moving mountains!"

"Leave him alone." Now my mother waved her hand at my father.

"Yeah," I muttered.

"I like mountains," yelled Nonna. "I lived near mountains when I was a little girl."

"He likes his theatre," said my mother.

"I know he does." He gave me a hearty slap on the back, which sent me flying forward. "But he's smart. Even Rob didn't get his grades."

Rob is my older brother. He's studying science at university. I'm the only one of us four boys who's into the arts, which makes me the weird one that no one really understands.

"He auditioned for Danny Zuko," said my mother.

"What's for dinner?" Nonna yelled.

"You should be proud of our boy," my mother said to my

father. "He's probably going to get the lead role from that movie *Grease*."

Oh no, I thought. This was getting worse by the minute. I liked that she was my champion but sometimes she needed to put her mama-bear routine on pause.

"You'll change how you think when you see him on the stage," she continued proudly.

I wanted to fall through the floor and into my room, land on my bed, and stay there until morning. Oh, but have my dinner delivered since I'd figured out that we were having homemade gnocchi.

"You know, the one with John Travolta and Olivia Newton-John," she said, just keeping at it like a bloody skipped CD. "We saw it at the movie theatre years ago."

She turned to Nonna and said loudly, "Gnocchi." Then she pointed to her ears. "You need to turn them up."

"*Grease*—I remember that movie," said my father. "I liked it." He puffed out his chest and I had to look away. The peacock-man-chest was something I was totally lacking. I wondered how I was going to get out of this conversation. "Didn't they drive the hot rod cars at the end?"

Okay, I caught a break, I thought. *He loves cars.* "I've heard they're bringing in a real car for the set. Someone loaned a vintage Cadillac to the school."

"A vintage Cadillac would have a V8 engine." He nodded as if he knew everything about everything about cars.

Thankfully the twins, Jason and Jerrod, dressed in jerseys and soccer shorts, burst into the kitchen, sliding on the hardwood floor. The noise escalated above even Nonna, and for once I was happy that they were annoying.

"When are we eating?" Jerrod asked. Although they were fourteen, they looked like they were twelve and acted like they were eight. They complained about being late developers and how it didn't help their soccer but I envied them their still-lithe bodies. Sometimes, I wished I could be back there again, before puberty, before my hormones kicked in and turned everything upside down

"I asked that too," said Nonna. "No one answered me. No one ever answers a damn thing in this house."

My mother turned and waved her spoon at Nonna. "No cussing in this house. I said we're having gnocchi."

Nonna plunked herself down at the table, in her designated seat. "Damn, damn," she muttered.

"Ten minutes," said my mom.

"Gianni auditioned for *Grease* today," said my mom to Jerrod and Jason.

"As if they care." I muttered under my breath. Surprise, surprise; their facial expressions didn't change. Why my mother thought they would be remotely interested in my life was beyond me. All they cared about was soccer and food and, honestly, we were like distant relatives instead of siblings.

My dad put his arm around me and squeezed my shoulder. "I'll come watch you, son."

"Thanks, Dad."

He released me and undid the knot in his tie. "That Travolta guy who played in that movie, isn't he in the magazines for being queer?"

The twins guffawed, like literally, by slapping their legs and laughing like idiots.

Well, that was my cue to leave.

Downstairs, I quickly walked by Rob's room even though he was the one person in my family, besides my mother, who I actually conversed with. Today I was so done talking about the audition and I just wanted to hide. I wasn't getting the part. I could have *acted* out the romance between Sandy and Danny and I could have *acted* the macho guy. I could have if they'd have given me a chance.

As soon as I entered my room, I shut my door and flopped on my bed to stare up at the ceiling.

How was I going to do this for almost two more years?

I knew what I was, or I thought I knew what I was, and I'd known since I'd hit puberty, or I thought I'd known since puberty. Did I know before the hormones kicked in? I'd have to say I don't think so because I was just a kid who tried t-ball and soccer but excelled at basketball and also liked music. But once my body started to change, all bets were off.

Girls were not on my radar.

Boys were.

I noticed their bodies, their mannerisms. And I spent time on my computer Googling gay athletes and gay celebrities and reading blogs and Q and A's about "How to Know?"

The confusion was killing me, the secret even more, but to maintain my sanity and keep our household from blowing the roof off, I was determined to keep my inner thoughts and feelings a secret until I left this house, this city, and my high school.

I rolled over and stuck my face in my pillow.

CHAPTER FIVE
ERIKA

"**I** don't want to get up," I said. The knock on my door came every morning at 7:00 am. And I didn't get up. I liked being under my warm comforter.

"Erika," said my mother, "you're going to be late."

"What-*ever*."

"Remember, you don't like being late."

"NO." I pulled the covers up past my chin. "I'll only get up if you play my game."

"Knock, knock," said my mother.

"Who's there?" I asked again, pulling my blanket even higher.

"Orange," said my mother.

"Orange you glad it's not banana?" I covered my face with my blanket and laughed.

My mother opened my door and said, "Okay, Erika, now it's really time to get up."

"*What-ever.* But on Saturday I don't have to get up."

"Okay, it's a deal," said my mother. "On Saturday when there's no school you can sleep in. I promise."

"*It's a deal. It's a deal.*"

I frowned at my mother as I got out of bed, squishing my eyebrows together.

Every night before bed, I put the clothes I'm going to wear the next day on a chair. But before I get dressed I always have to go to the bathroom first. I walked across the hall to the bathroom I share with Karina, and my legs still felt like they wanted to sleep. And my eyes too.

Once I was dressed in my jeans and a pink t-shirt, I walked out of my bedroom and down the hall to my mom and dad's room. Every morning I go to see my dad before I eat my breakfast. I have to say goodbye. Yup. I do.

But I didn't have to feed him in the morning because I had to go to school. Every morning I have a routine and I call it my Groovy Groove. And I don't like when it changes. No Siree.

"Knock, Knock."

My dad didn't answer with 'Who's there?' though. I opened the bedroom door and peeked inside. I saw his body lying like a big lump on the bed. The light was off in his room so I walked as quietly as I could over to his bed and kissed his cheek.

"Good morning," he said, without opening his eyes. His voice sounded funny, barky and scratchy, and not very loud.

"Today there will be a *list* for *Grease*." This list would be a piece of paper put on the bulletin board with a tack. If the teachers wanted me to sing and dance, my name would be on the *list*.

"A list?" His voice still sounded low and kind of funny like he couldn't breathe.

"I want to dance on stage. But my name has to be on the *list*."

"Fingers crossed," he said with a cough.

"You can't cross your fingers," I said. I pulled up his covers. "Go back to sleep."

"I love you," he said.

"I love *you* to the moon and back," I said. I always say that. I like saying that. I learned that from a movie.

Then I left his room, closing the door so he could go back to sleep until Shelley came over or Antonio.

On the weekdays, I eat my cereal with milk because my mother says it's good for my bones. It makes me strong. Before she leaves for work she makes my turkey sandwich, (I like eating the same thing every day, every day) and puts two cookies and an apple in my lunch bag.

My cereal didn't taste very good because my tummy was going up and down again and around and around too. I had another *upset stomach*. The list was going up today. *The list.* This was my first time waiting to see a *list* that might have my name on it. I had only eaten half my cereal when Karina came into the kitchen.

"Erika," she said in her hurried voice, "I'm going to put the timer on and when it rings you need to be finished your breakfast."

"*What-ever.*" Karina likes to put me on a timer so we won't be late because she drives me every morning. Well, not every day. Sometimes Karina goes early and on those mornings my mother drives me on her way to work.

I slurped my cereal, *slurp, slurp,* until the timer went off, then I tipped my bowl and drank all the milk before I took my bowl to the dishwasher. Now I had to brush my teeth.

Karina walked by the bathroom when my mouth was full of toothpaste. "Are you almost done? We're going to be late if you don't speed things up." She shook her head. "I should have put the timer on for this task too."

I spit the toothpaste in the sink. "I'm a slowpoke."

She squinted and her eyes looked small. "Why do you keep saying that?"

"Mrs. Barr tells me that in phys ed. Sometimes it takes me *soooo* long to get dressed."

"We need to get your aid to help you get dressed then. I'll talk to Miss Saunders. Wipe the toothpaste off your mouth and I'll get your coat and hat."

Miss Saunders is my aid who helps me at school. Sometimes she walks me to class or comes to class with me. But not all the time. Nope. I don't need her all the time.

In the back hallway, Karina handed me my coat and I put it on, then I put on my plaid tam hat, my most favourite hat. When I started high school I didn't like going. Lots of mornings I sat on the kitchen floor and wouldn't get up. I cried too. *Wah, wah, wah.* Karina and my mom didn't like it when I did that. No Siree. I couldn't help it. Walking so much at school made me tired and made my legs feel like big rocks. But now I like it better because I know where to go. I'm not late very often, except when I have to change for phys ed. *Gross* phys ed.

"When do you find out about the musical?" Karina fixed my hat, tucking my hair so it wasn't in my face.

"I dunno. There will be a *list.*"

"Do you know what a list is?" Karina put her hand on my back and moved me toward the door.

"Well, *duh*, yeah. It's a piece of paper Mr. Warner and Miss Clark put on the bulletin board with a tack. If I get to sing and dance, my name will be on it."

"Wow. I'm impressed. Big day for you. Remember, you have a Best Buddies meeting after school too."

"Well, duh. It *is* the first Thursday of the month."

She kept moving me toward the door. "I wish you wouldn't say that one. I don't know who you learned it from but it's annoying. Let's get your backpack. It's right there by the door."

"I like saying it. Well, duh. I need my lunch too," I said.

Karina waved my blue lunch kit in the air. "Well, duh," she said. "I've got it."

"You said it too!" I laughed.

When we arrived at school, Karina walked me to the front door and then she told me to go to my locker. I know how to get to my locker and how to get to my first class. Miss Saunders, my aid, usually meets me at my locker. She takes me to most of my classes but I go to drama and art and sometimes phys ed by myself. *Gross* phys ed. I like it when we dance and I don't have to change. It takes me too long to get into *stoopid* gym clothes.

On my very first day of school, last year, I was with Miss Saunders and she wanted me to sit with her and I told her No Way José. I wanted to sit with all the other kids and the *boys*. She laughed when I said that to her and she sat in the back and I sat with everyone else so that made me like Miss Saunders.

Miss Saunders was waiting for me at my locker.

"Hi, Erika."

"What's shakin', Miss Saunders?"

"What's shakin' is *you* have science first. You will need to get your science notebook and textbook from your locker. You're working on an experiment today."

I couldn't say *well duh* to Miss Saunders. My mother had told me to never say that to any teacher at school. Instead, I said, "I like *ex-per-i-ments* better than listening."

"I get that," she said. "Most students do."

I didn't want to think about science today when the *list* was going up at lunch. "Guess what?" I asked her.

"What?" She eyed me to see if I was going to tell her a joke but I wasn't, not right now. "Today I find out about *Grease*. My name will have to be on a *list*."

"That's great, Erika!" She raised her eyebrows up and down. "I heard from a little birdie that you rocked your audition." She held up her thumbs.

"Yeah, I *rocked it*." I liked *that* saying. "*Rocked*," I said the word again. This time I giggled and put my hand to my mouth.

Miss Saunders laughed too. "It's a good expression for you. And a new one. Always good to have new sayings."

"I like new sayings."

"Yes, you do. Now, come on," said Miss Saunders, "let's get a move on. We need to get to class." We walked down the hall together but I stopped walking when I saw Gianni.

"Cool shirt, Erika. Pretty in Pink." He held up his thumb. "Rumour is they're putting up the list at lunch."

"Lunch?" I looked up at him. That was only two classes away.

"That's what I heard."

"We *rocked* it," I said. I waited for him to laugh but he didn't. *Boo hoo.* Maybe he had an upset stomach and felt sick like me because of the *list*.

"*You* rocked it, girl." He winked and pointed his finger at me but he wasn't smiling today. Usually he smiles a lot.

"Can you meet in the drama room?" he asked. "Or do you want me to walk you?"

"Well duh, I can get to the drama room."

"Of course you can." He looked at his watch. "I gotta run to math," he said. "See you at lunch."

"Ciao for now," I said.

In science class we had to do an electricity experiment. We had to find out if a *current* was faster in a thick wire or a thin wire. At first I didn't know what a current was but Miss Saunders explained it to me. She also helped me understand thick and thin. I wondered if Gianni, because he was a skinny-minny, was thin? Miss Saunders said it was kind of a good way to look at it but it wouldn't be polite to tell people they were thin or thick.

Miss Saunders sat with me the whole experiment so she was my partner. I wanted to have a boy for a partner like Crystal had. Crystal and Max were partners. I like doing experiments *waaaay* better than listening to a teacher talk. Sometimes if the teacher just talks and talks and talks, the words just go on and on and on and I get mixed up. Teachers tell my parents I learn better when I do something and, yup, that's me-to-a-tee.

As we were working with the thick wire, I heard two girls talking about how they wanted to *cel-e-brate* if they got a part in *Grease*. I wanted to *cel-e-brate* too. I did, I did. Then one girl said it would be classic if Richard Temple got the big part. *Classic*. That was a new word. I liked how it sounded.

"Erika," said Miss Saunders. "Let's try to see if this will work, okay? Then I want you to fill out this sheet."

She put a sheet of paper in front of me that had questions on it. I didn't want to fill out the sheet. I looked at the questions and they looked hard. I pushed it away from me.

"Erika, it's okay. I'll help you. By the end, I bet you understand. Look at these two wires. Which one is thicker?"

All morning I had a hard time concentrating on school because everyone was talking about the *list*. All the talk made my tummy feel as if it was going to explode like a firecracker. Once when I was seven years old we went to a fireworks display on July 1st for Canada Day and the fireworks *popped, popped,* in the air. My dad held me up on his shoulders so I could see, but the popping was so loud I had to cover my ears. My dad held my legs as hard as he could so I wouldn't fall to the ground and hurt myself. His hands still worked when I was seven and I didn't like that they didn't work now. It makes my heart hurt, like a needle keeps pricking it. My mom and Karina tell me not to think about him being so sick, like I'm not supposed to think about needles when I go to the doctor.

At lunch break, I twirled my lock around and around, and when it clicked open, I put my books away and got out my blue kit that kept my sandwich cold. The halls were filled with kids getting their lunches so I had to walk slow. Then I saw Crystal and Max kissing, *right in the hallway.* I wanted to kiss a *boy*. Karina told me to stop looking at her when she kissed Cameron, so I stopped looking at Crystal and Max. I kept walking and walking. It took me a long time to get to the drama room.

Gianni was in the drama room when I got there and he still wasn't smiling. Sometimes Karina calls me a sourpuss when I don't smile. Kids were standing in front of the bulletin board and I saw the white paper. The *list*.

"*Grease* Cast List." I read it out loud.

"Congrats, Erika!" Sonya held up both her thumbs. "You made it!"

I jumped up and down and up and down and my heart

went *cra-azy* and then I couldn't breathe so I had to stop jumping.

"Are you okay?" Sonya asked.

"I can feel my heart," I said, putting my hand to my chest. It was beating and beating. "I wanna see my name!"

Sonya put her hands on my shoulders and moved me around some of the other kids so I could stand right in front of the bulletin board. I stared up at it. When I saw my name, *Erika Wheeler*, I clapped my hands.

"You get to sing and dance in *three* numbers," said Sonya.

"Three numbers!" I cheered putting my hands in the air as if I was at a basketball game.

"I'm so happy for you," said Sonya.

I stopped cheering and looked back at the list. At the top, I saw that Sonya was Sandy. I turned and hugged her. "You're Sandy! You're going to be the best Sandy."

"Richard got the part of Danny," Sonya whispered in my ear. "You should go talk to Gianni. He's been cast as Eugene."

"That's *classic* that Richard got the part," I said.

"What do you mean by that?"she asked, squishing her eyebrows together.

"I dunno."

"Don't say that to Gianni, okay?"

I looked down at the floor. Did I say something wrong? The girls had said it in science class. No one said *they* shouldn't.

"Erika, it's okay," said Sonya. She used her finger to lift my chin. "I've got an idea. Why don't you go over and tell him you're in three songs? That will make him happy."

I walked over to Gianni and tugged on his jacket to get him to turn and see me. "I'm in *three* songs," I said, holding up my fingers to show three.

"Way to go!" He held up his hand and I high-fived him. "I told you you could do it," he said.

After we had high-fived, he shoved his hands in the pockets of his jeans.

"You're not Danny," I said.

He shrugged. "It's okay."

"Eugene's funny." I'd watched the movie so many times and I liked Eugene.

Gianni smiled but it wasn't a real smile. It was like the smiles the girls in grade six gave me when they wanted to baby me, instead of be my friend. In grade six I played with the boys because they didn't act like my mother and try to baby me and treat me like a baby doll. *Wah, wah, wah.* I didn't want to be a baby doll.

"Are you going to cry?" I asked Gianni. "You look sad. Like the puppy I saw at the Humane Society. My mother wouldn't let me get it cuz my dad's sick. It's okay to cry when you're sad."

"I'm proud of you," he said. "I'll help you learn the dance steps."

"*Awe-some,*" I said.

Gianni stopped looking at me when a boy named Bilal Hakim walked in the room. I knew Bilal's family was from a country called *Leb-a-non* and I always remember that even if I don't know where it is. I don't like maps. He played soccer and was tall but wasn't *thin* like Gianni. I think skinny-minny sounds better.

"I'm going to talk to Bilal for a few seconds," said Gianni. "Okay?"

"Yup."

Gianni left me alone and I stood there staring and looked at all the people who would be in *Grease*. My insides were bubbling like I was a soda drink. My mom only let me have soda drinks on special days. This bubbling inside me made me happy and it wasn't like when I had to audition. No Siree! These were happy bubbles. I was going to be part of the musical and I was going to sing and dance in three numbers. I clapped my hands I was so happy, happy.

Three of the girls who were dancers stood together on the other side of the room, over by Mr. Warner's messy desk. Piled papers looked like they could topple off. One girl who had red hair, Amanda Carlson, danced all the time. She went to my other school. In grade eight for the talent show, she jazz danced and wore a leotard and black slipper shoes and won a ribbon. I did the moonwalk and wore a real black hat and they gave me a special award. I put it on my dresser.

There was another girl there too. She had short brown hair and brown skin, and her name was Suzanne Singh. She was in my science class but I didn't know if she took dance classes like Amanda. No Siree. I didn't know the third girl and she was on her cell phone. I wanted a cell phone. But my mother said I had to show her I could use it *pro-per-ly* and not just play games.

I walked over to them.

"Hey, Erika. Congrats," said Amanda.

"Yeah, congrats," said Suzanne.

The other girl I didn't know stopped talking on her phone and pressed the button to end her phone call. I knew where that button was. Then she said, "Hi Erika, my name is Claire." She crinkled her nose when she smiled at me and I thought she was pretty like Liesl in *The Sound of Music*. I liked the part when she sings that she's sixteen going on seventeen. One day I would be sixteen and I wanted to dance with a *boy* like Liesl did.

They started talking again. I stared at Claire's cell phone. It was pretty cuz it was purple. If I got a cell phone, I wanted a purple one too.

"Let's meet at the dance studio early, before class. There's never anyone in the back studio at that time," said Amanda. "Miss Clark wants me to help with the choreography. I want to make it *wow*." She used her hands to talk and I liked how long her fingers were and her pink nail polish. "Lots of hand jive, swing dancing, cha-cha—you know, fifties stuff," she said.

"That's doable for me," said Suzanne. "I can help. Do you think we could throw in some tap?"

Amanda clamped her lips together and I knew she was thinking so I didn't say anything. My mom did that. Amanda tapped her feet on the floor. *Tap. Tap.* "Not everyone has tap shoes, so I doubt it," she said.

I don't have tap shoes, I thought inside my head. *And I don't have a cell phone.*

"Just a thought." Suzanne shrugged. "But we can use our jazz backgrounds for sure to liven up the dances."

"I learned some hand jive at a dance workshop last year," said Claire.

I wanted to say 'me too' but I'd never done those dances before. I'd only ever learned how to waltz with Gianni. My mother told me not to lie.

"I can waltz," I said. "And do the moonwalk."

Claire grinned. "I loved your moonwalk at your audition."

"I *rocked* it," I said.

They laughed and that made me happy because I had a new thing to say.

Amanda looked at the clock on the wall. "We better get going or lunch will be over. See you later, Erika," said Amanda. She patted my head.

"Let's go celebrate," Amanda said to Claire as she hooked her arm in hers and walked away from me.

I watched them walk away but they stopped after a few steps.

"We need a selfie," said Amanda.

She held up her phone and Amanda and Claire and Suzanne smiled in it. I watched. I wanted to be in the selfie. I had taken them on Karina's phone so I knew how.

They walked away and I stood by myself even though I wanted to be in the selfie and go celebrate. My heart hurt again, like it was being pricked, but not as much as it did for my father. I had to be invited; my mother told me that. Why didn't they invite me? I was going to sing and dance too.

My lunch was still in my lunch kit and soon it would be time for drama class. I walked over to Gianni who was talking to Bilal.

"Do you want to eat lunch with me?" I asked Gianni.

He turned and looked at me before he looked around the room. "Where are the other girls?"

"They left." I hung my head and stared at my feet and suddenly I didn't feel like I did when they had laughed after I said I *rocked* it. My eyes started stinging.

"I'll eat with you," he said. "I bet you have a better lunch than me."

I looked up and he smiled at me, so I smiled back.

Together, Gianni and I walked out of the drama room and down the hall to the lunch room. He always walked beside me, and not in front of me like Karina.

"What's a hand jive?" I asked.

"Remember when we took ballroom dancing for the Best Buddies Halloween party and we learned the waltz?" He asked.

"Yup," I said. "I *rocked* it."

Gianni laughed. "The hand jive is another type of dance. Only faster. Next time you watch *Grease* on television, watch when they dance in the high school gym."

I thought about how much they danced in the movie.

"You thinking?" he asked.

I nodded. Finally, I said, "They dance a lot."

He stopped walking. "You're right. You won't know which one is the hand jive just by watching." He looked up and down the hallways. "It will be better if I show you. But I will just show you the basic hand movements, okay? There are five of them. Watch closely."

"In the hallway?" I asked.

"It's empty," he said.

He was being serious so I had to *fo-cus.*

"First move is tapping your thighs." He slapped his hands on his legs so I did the same thing.

"Now, clap, that's an easy one," he said.

"Easy-peasy," I said.

"Okay, so after that you cross your hands over each other in front of your body." He showed me that one and I followed.

"Now for a fun one—do hammer fists." He put his hands in fists and hammered one on top of the other.

"I like this one," I said. I did the hammer move.

"Me too." He winked. "But hold on to your hat, this last move is the best. Pretend to throw your thumbs over your shoulders."

I giggled and did exactly what he did.

"Do you follow?" he asked, raising his eyebrows.

I nodded. I was good at remembering things.

"Let's do eight of each."

Gianni went really slow and we went through the five moves eight times and we did it twice and I never flubbed once. I like the word flub. It starts with an F. I'm not supposed to say the other F-word. Lots of kids do though. I learned flub from Sonya because she flubbed a science test once.

"Now let's do four and speed it up," said Gianni.

Doing four was way harder, especially because we were going faster.

"It's okay," he said when I flubbed. "It's easier with music."

"One more time." I held up one finger.

"Sure."

We were on the clapping part when three big boys walked by and started laughing. "Ohhh, Gianni. You look so cute doing that with your *friend*."

Gianni stopped his clapping and didn't finish. "Come on, Erika." He put his hand on my back and pushed me forward. "Let's go to the cafeteria."

He walked so fast to get away from the boys and it was hard to walk that fast. I didn't like those boys. Not one bit. Karina had told me to stay away from them and they weren't very nice. She said they didn't like kids who were different and I knew I was different. I was born with Down syndrome and have an extra gene. I tried to walk as fast as Gianni to get away from the mean boys. My jeans rubbed together and made scratchy noises. *Scritch. Scratch.* Gianni never walked faster than me, but today he did.

CHAPTER SIX
GIANNI

E*ugene?*
Are you kidding me?

I stared at the list and just kept staring. Was I reading it wrong? But no. There it was. The word Eugene was typed, then there was a space...then there was my name, hand written. I swear my heart stopped beating and I died for a moment when I saw that I was Eugene. How could Mr. Warner do this to me? And Miss Clark too. She'd always had my back. Had I blown the audition that badly?

At least they could have cast me as Kenickie, or Doody, who got to sing with his guitar. They knew I could play the guitar for god's sake because I'd done it in the talent show last year. I scanned the list to see that beautiful Bilal had nabbed the part of Kenickie and I had to admit, he would do a good job. With his Lebanese background, he definitely had the swarthy, hot look that suited Kenickie.

I closed my eyes for a second to gather myself. Honestly, anyone but Eugene. Well, the Teen Angel would have sucked worse because you're in and out in a flash. Damn. I had wanted to snag the lead role. But oh no, of course, as soon as the star athlete stepped on the stage, (no matter how talented he was), he got the part. I used to be a basketball player. Okay, so I wasn't first string but I played in at least half the games in my first year of high school and won the Most Improved Player at the end of the year.

I forced myself to scan the rest of the list, breathing a sigh of relief when I saw that Erika was in the chorus for three songs—not two but *three*. They were going to let her take the stage for the beginning number, the last number and also the prom number. She even got a costume change. Good for her.

Sonya's name was beside Sandy. To me, she was the best choice.

I felt a little tug on the sleeve of my jacket and turned to see Erika, her excited face lifting my spirits.

"I'm in three dances!" She squealed and jumped up and down.

"I know!" For her sake I had to be excited.

She tilted her head and stared up at me. "You're not Danny."

"It's okay," I said.

"Eugene's funny."

I tried to smile. I did.

"Are you going to cry?" she asked. One thing about Erika, she was great at reading facial emotions, well any emotions really. It was astonishing how sometimes she knew exactly how I was feeling when I thought I was covering quite well. Heat flushed my face.

"I'm proud of you and I'll help you learn the dance steps," I said.

Last thing I wanted was to talk about my pathetic sadness. Or cry in the drama room. I turned from her for a second and that's when I saw Bilal on the other side of the room. My heart quickened and electricity flowed through my entire body at the sight of him. Like Richard, he was a weight-room junkie and on the soccer team. He lifted his hand and gave me the smallest wave and I thought I would pass out on the spot, crumble at the knees like a puppet whose strings had been snipped. I responded to the gesture with my own little wave. Should I walk over? He was the one who'd waved first. Should I?

Do it.

I quickly excused myself from Erika because I had to act before I lost my nerve. Erika would be fine on her own for a few moments and, anyway, she now was part of a cast, a soon-to-be family.

A few moments later, I stood beside Bilal. Suddenly I felt awkward and embarrassed, but every nerve in my body was ignited and zapping me. I quickly glanced at Erika and saw her with some of the other dancers. Good. I could concentrate on Bilal.

"Congrats," I managed to get one word out of my mouth.

"Thanks. Congrats to you too. Eugene is a good part."

"Yeah, for sure." Three words this time and no shaking voice. Now that's what I called progress.

"Richard might need help," he said, after a minute or so.

"I hear ya."

"I heard you had a great audition." He sounded sincere.

"Thanks for saying that."

Our shoulders brushed and electricity raced through me. I could hardly breathe, my throat was so dry. Did he touch me on purpose? I glanced at his face, trying to see if I could find the answer, wondering if he felt the same, or anything, toward me or if I was imagining things. Shouldn't I instinctively know who was or who wasn't?

"Do you want to eat lunch with me?" Erika asked. She dropped her head.

"Where are the other girls?" I looked around the room, which was now just about empty.

"They left," she said in a small voice.

Her body language spoke dejection and it broke my heart. Why couldn't they include her? She rarely got invited to birthday parties or out and no one thought it hurt her but it did. From what Karina told me the invites stopped around grade six.

"Sure," I said to her, lifting her chin with my finger and smiling at her. "I'll eat with you. I bet you have a better lunch than me." I was just about to ask Bilal to join us too when he touched my arm. "Later."

Later. *Later.* Had I heard right? Did he seriously just say *later*? Did he mean later as just an expression or later, like really *later* he wanted to talk to me again.

Right then, I knew I was going to keep reliving him saying that all night.

I watched him walk out the door before I made a move to leave with Erika.

Erika and I plodded down the hall together, side by side. Her steps echoed in the empty hallway. One thing I'd learned with Erika was to slow down my pace to a stroll, and, of course today, the slowness of the walk allowed my mind to wander to thoughts of Bilal.

"What's a hand jive?" Erika asked me.

Thank you, Erika. I needed to *not* obsess, which I was clearly doing. Right there in the hallway, I demonstrated the five moves and her eager face was the best distraction ever. We went through eight counts then four. With time and music she would get it no problem. She had a natural feeling for music and sometimes it just took her a little longer to grasp everything. We had just finished the leg-pat part when I heard footsteps.

"Ohhh, Gianni." The mocking tone was familiar. "You look so cute doing that with your *friend*."

I stopped clapping, and turned to stand in front of Erika, blocking her view of them. My cheeks burned. I had to get her away from these guys.

"Come on, Erika." I put my hand on her back and guided her forward. "Let's go to the cafeteria."

We walked away and I wondered if they were staring at us or if they had moved on to find their next victims. That lot was bad news, having somehow found each other this year, banding together to create an evil Gang of Four, slinging around racial slurs and homophobic comments whenever they could.

Just before Halloween, the youngest one in the group had cornered one of the Best Buddy members, Harrison Henry, and taken his lunch. Cowards. Fortunately, Justin, the Best Buddies Chapter President had stepped in, but not before the kid had made an impression on the older guys. He was in grade nine and it was like it was his big moment, his rise to fame. It made him part of the gang—and it made my stomach sick.

My gut instinct told me their bullying was escalating, and stealing a lunch was now kiddie's play. What would be next? Who would be next?

When the final bell rang, I packed up my books and headed to the utility room. I waited at the door for Erika so we could go in together. For the first Best Buddies meeting, I had walked with her but now she insisted on coming by herself.

"I'm in three songs," she said, holding up three fingers.

"I know," I said. "Good on ya."

Anna and Harrison, two other Best Buddy members, were already there. Anna waved at us but Harrison kept his head down; he had high-functioning autism and a brilliant brain that never stopped but lacked a few social skills.

There were two seats at the front, close to Willa and Gloria. I didn't know either of them well but did know Willa was a bit of a rocker, sporting a few tattoos and piercings, and Gloria had Fetal Alcohol Syndrome.

Don and Marcie sat a few rows back. Like Erika, Don was born with Down syndrome. He loved basketball. Marcie was on the high school basketball team so Mrs. Beddington had paired them together. Most of the pairs had something in common. Stuart and Sarah liked cooking. Anjana and Johana were into Star Wars. Ciara and Mohammed liked cartooning. The mix was good and the group was fun.

"I hope we have a dance," said Erika.

"I think it will be something different," I said.

Justin, the chapter president, was at the front. I pointed to the desks beside Gloria and Willa.

"Take a seat everyone," said Justin from the front of the room. "We should get started."

I liked how Justin ran our meetings, short and sweet, always getting to the point. He was the only one in the room without a Best Buddy for some reason.

"I think we should discuss our next event," said Justin.

"Does anyone have any ideas?"

"I read where some Best Buddies groups have a Hooping It Up event," piped up Willa. Willa rarely talked so I turned to look at her.

"I love basketball," said Don. He threw his hands in the air.

"I'm with ya, Don," said Justin.

"They invite the whole school," continued Willa, "and everyone takes turns shooting on the baskets and there are prizes and crap. I thought to give the event some spice, we could have a band play."

"Like a rock band?" Stuart asked.

"Yeah, why not?" said Willa, chewing her gum with total attitude. "My band could do it. For free," she added, blowing a bubble.

So that was the catch. One thing about Willa, she stayed true to who she was so, naturally, she would try to get the rock stuff in there. I liked that about her. She didn't care who thought what about her. I ran my hand through my hair and exhaled. Could I be like that one day? *Totally* be like that?

"I like the idea of a Hooping It Up event," said Justin, "but we'd have to think about the band idea. It might be a bit loud for some."

Willa shrugged. "Just a thought."

"Background music is good," I said. "Maybe you could just tone it down a bit, Willa."

"The band could add life," said Marcie. "I'm sure we could get some local businesses to help with prizes. Don and I would definitely be game for basketball, right Don?"

"You bet!" her Buddy answered.

Justin held up a sheet. "We need to form a committee."

"I wanna sign up," said Erika.

I shook my head, leaned into her, and whispered, "We won't have time with *Grease* rehearsals. Anyway, we helped with the last dance."

Justin held up his hand. "Oh, by the way everyone, a big congrats is in order. Both Erika and Gianni have been cast in the school musical."

Everyone in the room clapped and cheered.

"I'm in three songs." Erika held up three fingers for everyone to see.

"That is so awesome," said Anjana. Then she said, "Hey, I've got an idea. Why don't we all plan to go to the musical? We could buy tickets for the same night and sit together to support Gianni and Erika. We could make that an event night too."

Erika turned to me. "Everyone is coming to see us."

Yeah, including my family, I thought. *How the heck am I going to break it to my mom that I didn't get the lead?*

As soon as the meeting was over I walked Erika to her mom's car and said goodbye before I headed to my car.

The wind howled through me and I pulled my collar up.

A voice sounded from the distance. "Hey, loser, where ya going?"

I recognized it immediately. It was the youngest kid in that Gang of Four. His voice had barely started changing.

Seconds later, and like a pack of wolves, the rest of them were all around me. My heart pounded like a metronome out of control.

"Keep going, Kyle," said one guy to the kid. I could tell by his tone he was sneering. "We told you, he's yours."

"Where ya going?" Kyle squawked again.

"Home." I managed to spit out the word, hoping I sounded braver than I felt.

"Where's your sidekick? Your *girlfriend*." He laughed. "The two of you are like a circus show. Guys like you are a waste of skin." He spat on me.

"Is he even a guy?" One of the other guys laughed.

"You hang out with a *retard*." He gave an evil laugh.

"Don't you call her that!" This time I didn't have a problem getting my words out.

"Aww. Isn't that cute? Hey, Kyle, maybe we should check out his junk to see if he's even a *man*." One of the guys moved toward me. He was built like a brick wall.

"Do it, Kyle."

My heart thwacked against my ribs. I had to get out of there. My Honda Civic stood just ten feet away. Kyle I could probably handle, but not the other three. Then I heard other voices in the parking lot. Should I yell?

The voices got louder and louder. Definitely a big group. Then I saw the expression in Kyle's eyes change.

"Let's split," said the big guy to Kyle. "Later, dude. Better damage."

By now the voices were close, like really close. The four guys backed away. Acting nonchalant with their hands in pockets and pants riding their butts, they meandered off. Like a bad odour disappearing.

I raced to my car and yanked my keys out of my jeans pocket but my hands were shaking so badly I dropped the keys on the ground. *Come on. You have to get in the car.* I snatched up the keys, opened the door, and jumped in, pressing the lock as soon as the door was shut. My heart was still pounding a million miles an hour.

Within seconds I peeled out of the parking lot, my wheels spinning. Once I was safe on the road, I breathed in and out, in and out, in and out. I wiped the sweat off my forehead. I was clammy and hot and freaked. Totally freaked. But, it was over. For now.

Tomorrow, I would park somewhere else, far away from my usual spot.

CHAPTER SEVEN
ERIKA

"**M**y name was on the *list*. Three songs!" I held up my fingers.

"Oh, Erika, that's wonderful," said my mother as I buckled up my seatbelt.

"'Alma Mater,' 'Shakin' at the High School Hop,' 'We Go Together.'" I started singing 'We Go Together.' After I sang *sha wadda wadda*, I put my hand to my mouth and giggled. Then I said, "Sonya is Sandy."

"I'm glad she got the lead," said my mother.

"Gianni showed me the hand jive."

"Good for him."

"He's Eugene. I hope Daddy can come. Just like my Best Buddies."

My mother put on her blinker and pulled away from the curb. Once she was driving in a straight line she said, "I hope he can too."

"He's going to get better and come watch me."

My mother blew air out of her cheeks. "Remember how we talked about this? Daddy can't get better, Erika."

I looked down at my lap, at my fingers, and wondered why the *im-port-ant* stuff from food wouldn't go to my father's hands. It wasn't ever going to go to his hands again. Why?

Stoopid ALS. And now it was starting not to go to his neck and his legs and his breathing too. I didn't get it.

"Should we talk about it again?" my mother asked softly.

I put my hands over my ears and shook my head and instead of saying No Way José or No Siree, I just yelled, "NO!"

After I ate my dinner, my mother told me to get ready because she was taking me to a meeting. I got in the car and sat in the front seat.

"I wanna take dance classes," I said to my mother. I'd been thinking and thinking about this.

My mother was driving and we were going to a meeting of the Down Syndrome Society. Today had been a busy day and I was pooped (I can say pooped this way) but my mother said the meeting would be good for me.

"What kind of dance class?" My mother asked.

"Jazz and tap."

"I think dance classes would be a good thing for you to do. Perhaps we can sign you up in January."

"I wanna do them now."

"But now that you're in three numbers in *Grease,* you might be busy."

I thought about that as my mother pulled into a parking spot and turned off the car.

We got out of the car and walked toward the front door of a grey building. I hoped they were serving chocolate chip cookies tonight instead of vegetables and dip. I don't like broccoli. It's *gross.* The parents drink coffee and I drink juice.

Sometimes I like coming to the meetings but other times I don't. Tonight I wanted to stay home with my father but my mother said that this was a good meeting to go to because it was about "Keeping Secrets." I didn't like the word *secret*; it made me have an upset stomach.

Inside the building there was a room we always went to when we had meetings and all the chairs were in a circle. I saw kids I knew because we'd been coming to this room since I was little. My dad used to come too, but after last time he said he was too tired. *Stoopid* ALS.

My friend, Jimmy Trembley, walked over to me and he wore jeans and a t-shirt and a baseball hat backwards. He wore it like that to be *chill*. He went to Central High School and he liked to run and was in the Special Olympics. I wondered if they had dancing in the Special Olympics because then I could be in it too, just like Jimmy. Some of the other kids at the meeting didn't go to a high school like me and Jimmy and they went to other schools.

"Hi, Erika," said Jimmy.

"What's shakin', Jimmy?"

He laughed. "You always say that."

"To Miss Saunders too. She's my aid."

"I have an aid too but not for phys ed cause I'm good at phys ed." He pounded his chest.

"I'm in *Grease*."

"*Grease*?" He pushed his eyebrows together.

"It's a musical. I get to dance in three songs." I held up three fingers.

"*Cool*," he said. "I ran track inside today because it was too icy to run outside. And then I did weights." He put his arm up so he looked like the Hulk. "Look at my guns."

"Those aren't guns."

"It means muscles," said Jimmy.

"I *au-di-tioned* with a mic."

Jimmy pushed his glasses up his nose because they always fell down. "I love talking in a mic."

"I covered my ears." I put my hands over my ears to show him. "It was *soooo* loud."

"Me too."

"I backed up." I showed him how I backed up. "I sang and did the moonwalk."

"I like your moonwalk." He laughed and pushed his glasses up his nose again.

I showed Jimmy my moonwalk.

He laughed again but he likes to laugh. Well, not all the time. Not when's he's running. And not when he loses. Then he stomps his feet. Once he fell to the ground and just lay there.

"I wanna try," he said.

We both did the moonwalk. He wasn't as good as me.

"My Best Buddy taught me how to do the hand jive today." I showed Jimmy the five moves.

"Let me try."

Jimmy learned fast like I did in the hallway. He liked the one where we threw our thumbs over our shoulders the best. Me too.

"I want cookies," I said, glancing at the snack table.

"I already had five." He held up his hand, spreading his fingers wide.

We walked over to the food and drink table. The plate of chocolate chip cookies sat on the table with the coffee and juice and I looked down at them. Two other friends were by the table.

Bryce and Jessica. Bryce talked in sign language and Jessica did too but she could talk a little but not as good as Jimmy and me. I went to speech classes with Jimmy. Bryce and Jessica were boyfriend and girlfriend and Bryce wore a hearing aid.

"I make in Home Ec," said Jessica. She pointed to the cookies.

She picked up two and gave one to Bryce. Then she turned to me and said, "Mawwy, Bwyce."

"You gettin' married?" Jimmy pushed his glasses up.

Jessica pulled Bryce close to her and kissed him!

My mother walked over to the table. "Um, Erika," she said. "The talk is about to start now."

"Bye," I said to Bryce and Jessica and Jimmy. They weren't kissing anymore. I walked over to the chairs with my mother.

From the front of the room a woman with long brown hair said, "Let's take our seats everyone."

"Come on," said my mom. "I'd like to sit at the front."

My mother and I sat down beside Jimmy and his father. The woman began talking and welcomed us to the meeting. She told us the meeting was about keeping secrets and she wanted us all to know that it wasn't good to keep secrets. I didn't like talking about secrets so I looked at my feet and swung them back and forth, back and forth. No Siree. No secrets for me. My mother put her hand on my knees and whispered, "People can't hear if you're kicking."

"I'm swinging," I said.

"Maybe you should stop so everyone can hear the speaker."

I crossed my arms and slouched in my chair. I looked away from her.

Next the woman handed out a paper that went around the room and we were supposed to take one. On the top of the page were the words 'good touches,' which I could read and then there were pictures. A boy named Aaron started making funny noises because he wore hearing aids. All of the touches were how Gianni and Sonya touched me, on my arm and back and head. Then the woman said if someone touched us in the wrong place we weren't to keep it a secret. The wrong place was in the private parts. I didn't show anyone my privates, ever. Not even in the bathroom. No Way José. My mother told me not to and Karina too and my dad too. It made me feel funny to think about someone touching me there so I looked at my feet.

Bryce who was sitting beside Jimmy tooted and it was loud. I started to giggle and put my hand to my mouth. Jimmy did too.

"He farted," said Jimmy, still laughing.

"Shhh," said Jimmy's father.

"You're supposed to say toot," I said to Jimmy. "Fart is another F-word."

"Erika, that's enough," said my mother quietly.

I swung my legs back and forth and watched my shoes move. What about other secrets? Ones that weren't bad-touching secrets?

I glanced over at Jimmy. Now he was tapping his feet on the tiles as he looked at the floor. I wondered if he was counting them. He liked counting things. He was a good runner because he was *ob-sessed* with how one time was faster than another time. He said he liked to zoom over the finish line.

Last year Jimmy liked a girl at his school and he told me and I told my sister, Karina, but she said I shouldn't go around telling everyone. Why not? I'd asked her. In her *uppity* voice, Karina had said that it was his *personal business*.

Was that a secret?

Like the woman was talking about?

Jimmy pushed his glasses up and stared at the woman so I looked at her too. She said that having a secret was like locking something up inside of you that kept twirling around. I didn't want anything locked up inside of me. That would be like having a gerbil in your stomach. No Way José. She kept talking and said it wasn't good to lock something up because it might make you sad or withdraw. *With-draw?* I didn't know that word but maybe it had something to do with the drawings. I did know the word sad. I didn't want to be more sad because my heart hurt already with my dad having stoopid ALS. *Stoopid* ALS. My mom said stoopid was a bad word so I only said it in my head. Karina said it wasn't as bad as the F-word.

At the end of the meeting, I didn't talk to my mother as we walked out the door. I was thinking too much about secrets.

In the car my mother asked, "Did you like the talk?"

"No," I said.

"Do you have any questions?"

"I don't know *with-draw.*"

"It means to not talk about something and become quiet. So if someone touches you in the wrong place you want to tell someone right away and not keep the secret to yourself. You always want to talk to me or Karina or Dad, okay?"

I wondered if my dad would still be up when I got home. We could watch *Grease* or I could read. Yup. I could. I was good at reading my *Forever After* book.

When I got home, Daddy was watching one of his shows

about people doing bad things like killing people. Those shows make me not feel very good in my tummy, and in my head too. Just like secrets. I kissed his cheek but didn't look at the television screen. My mother said I should do my homework at the kitchen table and let my dad watch his show, but my sister was downstairs in our big room with a *huge* television and she had friends over. I *loooved* it when she had friends over, especially boys, like Cameron who liked me.

"I wanna go downstairs," I said.

My mother looked up at our yellow-and-red kitchen clock. "Okay. You have until 8:30. Thirty minutes. Then it is time to do fifteen minutes of homework and get ready for bed. I will set the timer."

Once I was downstairs, I ran to the sofa and yelled out, "What's shakin'?" All Karina's friends turned and said hello to me. I jumped on the sofa and snuggled up beside Cameron, a tall boy who is skinny like Gianni and a basketball player. He had been at our house a million times. *Million*. It was a number with a lot of zeros. Karina and Cameron studied together in her *bedroom*. I couldn't have boys in my bedroom, even Gianni or Jimmy. *Boo hoo.*

"What's shakin', Cameron?"

"Not much, Erika," he said back. "How're you shakin' tonight?"

"I *rocked Grease*," I said. "I'm in three numbers." I held up three fingers. "'Alma Mater,' 'Shakin' at the High School Hop,' and 'We Go Together.'"

He laughed and I liked that he laughed at my new word. "I heard you rocked it," he said. "Everyone was talking about it at school today." He held up his hand and I high-fived it but then when I went low he followed and I tricked him by moving my hand away.

"You got burned," I said, laughing. I could do my trick tonight cuz I wasn't at school or somewhere like a meeting.

"I did." He laughed.

"Gianni's gonna help me dance," I said.

"That's perfect, Erika."

"I'm taking jazz too."

Karina looked at me and she squished her eyebrows together. "You don't take jazz. I would know because I would have to drive you."

I crossed my arms. "I'm getting signed up."

"That's news to me. I'm sure I'll be the last to know but the first to pick you up." She shook her head.

"Does Gianni have brothers?" Cameron asked me, and he was also squishing his eyebrows together like he was thinking.

"Three." I held up three fingers.

"I think I know Gianni's older brother," he said. "He graduated two years ago. I played basketball with him at a summer camp. He was such a great player and I remember being so intimidated because I was two years younger. But he was the nicest guy ever."

"I love Gianni," I said. "*He's* the nicest guy ever."

"Is he your *boyfriend?*" Cameron winked at me.

"No Way José!" Now it was my turn to squish my eyebrows together. "He's not my boyfriend. He's my Best Buddy."

"Cam, don't get her going." Karina grabbed a sponge ball off the floor and threw it at his head.

He laughed and ducked. The ball hit the wall.

"Okay, okay," he said. "I think he bats for the other side anyway."

"He doesn't play *baseball*," I said. "No Siree."

My sister got up and pretended to hit Cameron. I knew it was pretending because we were told not to hit people. "Stop confusing her," said Karina. Cameron held his hands in front of his face.

"Hey, I'm okay with it," said Cameron. "Seriously. To each their own. I even signed up to help the Pride Club at school." He tried to tickle Karina's stomach.

"I'm happy to hear that," she said.

He pulled her down on the sofa and continued to tickle her. I watched. He wasn't touching her privates, just her tummy and under her arms in her armpits. *Pee-Yoo.* Underarms are stinky. Gross. Yucky. And they need deodorant. She liked it and she laughed, so I giggled. She was laughing and laughing when she flung her arms and spilled a bowl of chips. *Ewwww.* Chips flew everywhere.

"Look what you made me do," she said, sitting up and brushing the hair out of her eyes.

Cameron helped her pick up the chips and throw them in the trash. Since there was another bowl on the table filled with orange Cheetos, I reached across and grabbed a handful. I crunched on my Cheetos, the noise loud in my head. *Crunch, crunch.* My fingers turned orange so I licked them as I stared at all Karina's friends. I counted five and licked one finger for each person. Cameron and Karina and Reid and Cassandra and Carly: three girls and two boys. Reid and Cassandra were looking at something on a cell phone. They kept looking at the cell phone. I wanted a cell phone too.

Cameron sat back down beside me. "I'm glad you have Gianni as a Best Buddy," he said.

"He *rocks*."

Cameron laughed at me cuz my new word was so *awesome*.

"He taught me the hand jive." I stood up. I did all five moves and never flubbed.

"Wow. That is so cool," he said. "I don't know how to do that." He paused for a second before he said, "You know how I said that about him batting for the other side?"

"You were being silly. He played *bas-ket-ball*. Not *baseball*. We might have a Hooping It Up event. You could win a prize!"

"Cool. I'll come if it's an open event." He looked at me and his eyes were serious like Gianni's when he's teaching me to *focus*. "Hey," he said, "you don't need to tell Gianni or anyone that I said anything about him batting, okay? He's a good kid. I didn't mean it." He tousled my hair. "Just keep that a secret. Between us."

A *secret?* I looked down at the flower pattern on the sofa.

Why was that a secret?

CHAPTER EIGHT
GIANNI

"I'm going out," I said to my mother. She slathered a bun with mayonnaise. Lunch condiments sat on the counter beside a big pile of ham because she insisted on making lunches at night.

"Where are you going?" she asked, keeping her knife moving.

"Out."

"Too vague." She plopped a piece of ham on the bun.

"Studying. With a friend." I paused. "A smart friend."

She waved her knife without looking up. "Away you go."

I walked over to her and kissed her on the cheek. "Thanks, Ma. I love you."

She lifted her head and gazed into my eyes for a second before she touched my cheek. "I love you too. Forever and always."

"Thanks," I said. I backed up a bit, then turned and headed out of the kitchen and out the door.

Outside, I sucked in a deep breath of cool fall air and ran to my car. I plugged in the address on my phone and turned on my GPS. I could do this.

My legs shook the entire drive and although I turned the heat on, I could not get warm. Still shivering, I pulled up in front of an old building with a white illuminated sign: Avenue Community Center. Behind the back of the building was a parking lot. I cranked the wheel and managed to find a spot.

And sat in my car.

And sat and sat.

Time ticked and ticked. Time. Something I thought about a lot. When was the right time? Wrong time? Would time help me?

You can do this, Gianni. Come on. Go.

But I couldn't open the door.

The meeting at the Community Center was an LGBT Support Group meeting. I had seen it advertised in the community events magazine. It started at 7:00. I watched the red numbers of my car clock. When 6:59 flashed, I put my hand on the door handle. The numbers flashed 7:00. Then 7:01.

Now it was too late and I couldn't possibly walk in late. Everyone would stare at me and I could kiss my anonymity goodbye because guaranteed that last seat in the back row was already taken.

I slouched and leaned back, closing my eyes. I thought this meeting might tell me if I was or wasn't, which of course was stupid because I did know and my feelings for Bilal were just making it so obvious. Two years seemed like a long time to wait for love when I wanted it right now.

No. Shut up, lie low. This coming-out stuff will be easier later. You need more time.

I started my car and peeled out of the parking lot. There was a Starbucks down the street where I could hang out and go over my *Grease* script to learn my lines until it was time to go home.

The first rehearsal for *Grease* started at 3:15 sharp on Monday afternoon, and when Miss Clark said sharp, she meant *sharp*. Mr. Warner was a little more lackadaisical and easy going so their combination as co-directors was a perfect match. I didn't want Erika to be late so I met her at her locker.

"You ready?" I asked. I hadn't seen her all day or all weekend.

She shut her locker but didn't look at me.

"What's wrong?" I asked.

She shook her head and her hair swung from side to side but she still didn't look at me.

"Something's wrong." I sang my words to see if that would help.

Nope.

Okay. So there was no *No Way José* or *No Siree*. "Is your dad okay?" I said softly, touching her on the shoulder.

She looked up at me as only she can do with her distinctive eyes, crinkly and warm. "He wants to see me dance."

"That's great," I said. I started walking to keep her moving.

"We watched *Grease* twice. Once Saturday and once Sunday." She held up two fingers, giving me the peace sign.

"He wouldn't want to miss you dancing and singing." I knew he had ALS but I hadn't seen him in at least three weeks so I wasn't sure if he was getting worse or not. Last time I'd seen him he'd been able to walk with canes but his body looked like a crumpled mess.

"My dad coughs and chokes."

His ALS had started in his thumbs and I guessed now was in his esophagus and possibly respiratory system and lower body too. "It's good you get to spend time with him on the weekend," I said.

"I read to him," said Erika.

"I bet he likes that." I kept her moving.

"Karina's friends came over last week," she said. "Cameron too."

From the side I could see her bottom lip sticking out and that was a clear indication that *something* was bothering her. Maybe Karina hadn't wanted her around when she had friends over? When Erika and I were paired together, I discovered that she and Karina were like normal siblings. They bugged each other and squabbled, and sometimes Karina wanted her to butt out, especially when she was with Cameron. They were a hot senior item in the school.

I touched her shoulder again to keep her moving forward. "Karina and Cameron are good for each other," I said. "They're both *brainiacs*." I hoped she would smile when I said *brainiacs* but she didn't.

"Not Cameron," she said. "He says silly things."

"What silly thing did he say?" I teased her a little.

She plodded down the hall.

Maybe she was nervous about the rehearsal and if she could do the dances. Cameron didn't seem like the kind of guy to say something hurtful. She was acting strange though. "I can help you with the dances," I said.

"I might take a dance class. Jazz or tap. My mom said only one." She held up one finger.

"Your mom is probably right."

I put my hand on her shoulder to keep her moving to the drama room. "We can't be late for the first rehearsal."

"I don't wanna be late," she said.

"Stick with me, kid." I winked at her and she wrinkled her nose and smiled. Finally, I had cracked her a little. I didn't want her to carry whatever was bothering her over to rehearsal, not on the first night. She needed every ounce of energy and focus she had to get through the rehearsals. We all did.

We managed to get there at exactly 3:13. The room was already full with cast members and as soon as I entered I saw Richard, and it hit me right in the solar plexus: the guy was athletic and hot and that could be a good reason for casting him as Danny. They had wanted the soccer stud to star because he could draw a crowd; jocks and cheerleaders would come, and flocks of girls from other schools.

I pointed to a spot at the table where there were two chairs. Tonight was a read-through so we were sitting. Erika followed me and we sat down. She sat beside Richard and he grinned at her and held up his hand. She high-fived him back with a big smile. Good. I wanted her happy at this first rehearsal because, with no lines, it could be long and boring for her.

Sonya sat across from me and she lowered her head and smiled at me, almost coyly, and I wondered if she was getting into being Sandy, her character. I flashed my best geeky Eugene smile, one that I had practised all weekend in front of the mirror, and she burst out laughing.

"Eugene." I raised my eyebrows up and down and slouched into my Eugene posture.

"You're going to kill it in that role."

"Here's hoping," I said.

Bilal sat down in the empty chair beside Sonya and my heart skipped, jumped, and pole vaulted a few beats before it sped up like a crazy race car. I tried to catch his eye but he ignored me, saying hi to Sonya, but not even glancing in my direction.

He leaned into Sonya, their shoulders touching, as if he was flirting with her. Was he doing this on purpose, for my sake, showing me something? Telling me to back off? Sonya reacted and from what I could see, flirted back, but she also glanced at me out of her peripheral vision. Did she want me to see her flirting with Bilal? Be jealous? Well, I was. I wanted Bilal to rub shoulders with me, not her.

"Congratulations, everyone!" Miss Clark broke me out of my thoughts.

The entire room burst into applause, including me, and suddenly I was glad I was in the musical. Eugene was going to help me forget about everything and allow me to be someone else, even if the guy was a complete nerd.

The read-through started with the Rydell High song right at the beginning of the script. Miss Clark looked at me. "Eugene, I want this to be your solo. Feel free to make it as big as you want."

I got a solo! I nodded. "Will do," I said.

Line by line, page by page, we went through the rest of the script. Erika sat quietly beside me and didn't kick her legs back and forth, which was a sign she was listening and not uncomfortable.

When we hit the last page, Miss Clark said, "That's a good start. I would like to work on some of the dance scenes next rehearsal. Once we have the routines I will add the singing."

"And I'm going to work on the blocking for the acting scenes," said Mr. Warner. "Check the rehearsal schedule."

"You're free to go," said Miss Clark. Then she said, "Gianni, I want to see you."

The rehearsal ended and I told Erika to wait for me so I could make sure she found Karina to get her ride home.

"Can I have your phone, please?" she said. "I can text her."

I handed her my phone. She often used it.

"Gianni," said Miss Clark, "I want you to help Erika learn the dance moves. I'm a little concerned about her handling three numbers. I added an extra number to give her a costume change to make her feel part of the show."

I looked over at Erika, who was happily occupied with my phone. I turned back to Miss Clark. "She can do three, trust me."

"Ok. I'll leave it with you. Thanks for your help with this."

"No problem."

As Erika and I were leaving the drama room, I said, "What did Karina say?"

"She's busy."

Just then, my phone pinged with a text from Karina, telling me she was running late and was still in some after-school Student Council meeting. I texted her back telling her not to worry and I would drive Erika home because we were done.

"You're coming with me," I said to Erika, stashing my phone in my jacket pocket.

"You're driving me?" She stared up at me.

"You bet."

"You could say hi to my dad."

"Sure," I replied.

We walked to my car and didn't talk much. I kept

glancing over my shoulder to see if anyone was following us. My stomach churned just thinking about what could happen if those four guys surrounded us.

"You parked far away," she said.

"We're almost there," I said in response.

Erika was tired by the time we got to my car. We were just out of the parking lot when she asked me, "Do you play baseball?"

Weird question. I glanced at her out of the corner of my eye. "I did when I was little. And sometimes I play fun games in the summer."

"Oh, good," she said. "So it's not a secret."

"Uh, no. It's not a secret. Who said it was?"

"Cameron."

"Cameron? Like Karina and Cameron? That Cameron?"

"My sister likes him."

"They're an item all right. I played t-ball with his brother." Cameron had probably been making small talk with her because I did play t-ball with his brother way back when.

"He said he played basketball with your brother," she said.

"Yeah, I think you're right on that one." I had no idea if she was right or not as I didn't know every kid who had played basketball with my brother.

"At summer camp."

"That's probably true. My brother used to do basketball camps to get ready for the school season."

"I don't like secrets," she said.

I was used to Erika's train of thought changing, but today she seemed really distracted. I had no idea why she was bringing up the topic of secrets now. Staring ahead at the road,

I sucked in a deep breath, holding the air in my lungs for a second before I exhaled. How was I to reply that I didn't like secrets either when my whole life felt like one big secret?

"I'm looking forward to seeing your dad." I had to say something to stop myself from dwelling on the confusing chitchat that was going on inside my brain. "What book are you reading to him now?"

"*Forever After.* And the Berenstain Bears cuz my dad likes them."

"I loved those books."

"They're sort of baby books."

"Not really," I said. We chatted about the Berenstain Bears books and Disney movies until I pulled up in front of her house. I got out, walked around the car, and opened the car door for her. "Watch your step, Miss." I said in my best British accent.

"I'm a *cel-e-brity.*" She giggled, putting her hand over her mouth. Every time she got out of my car, we played the same game. She stepped out of the car and curtsied.

I linked my arm in hers and we headed up her walk together. Once inside, we heard voices sounding from the family room and I figured it was her father watching television.

After Erika hung up her coat and I took off my shoes, she pulled my hand. "Come say hi."

My first reaction when I saw her father, sitting in his chair, was to try not to look or sound shocked by the changes in him. His nurse, whom I had met once before, started packing up her bag. For the life of me I couldn't remember her name and it made me realize I should be visiting him more, especially now.

"I need to get going." The nurse talked fast, sounding flustered. "My daughter has a dance class." She packed up her bag. "Karina was supposed to be here thirty minutes ago."

"I can stay," I said.

"That would be great."

"I'll see you tomorrow," she said to Mr. Wheeler.

He lifted his arm a little in an effort to wave. Last I'd seen him, he'd been walking with a cane. Was he confined to his wheelchair now?

"Hey, Mr. Wheeler," I said. "It's great to see you."

"Hi. Gianni." His speech had slowed.

"You must be proud of Erika," I said. Erika hopped on the sofa and plunked herself down beside her father, leaning her head so she could nuzzle her face into his arm.

"She had a great audition," I said.

He tried to touch her hand and the movement was so slow and shaky. I blinked slowly and swallowed. Erika just grabbed his hand, lifted it, and kissed the back of it.

"Daddy wants to see me dance," she said, stroking his hand.

"It's going to be a super show," I said with forced enthusiasm. "Erika is in three huge numbers and gets a costume change. We're going to practise hard." I winked at Erika. "Aren't we?"

"Yup!" she said.

"I'll…be there."

"I'm glad to hear that." A part of me wondered if that would be possible six weeks from now.

The back door slammed and Karina yelled, "Hey, I'm home!"

Waves of relief and guilt washed over me. I should be able to handle this for Erika's sake. "I should get going," I said.

Karina blew into the family room like a windstorm at its peak. "Thank you *soooo* much, Gianni. Did Shelley go?"

"Yeah," I said.

"Dad, are you okay? Do you need help with anything? With Gianni here we could transfer you to the sofa."

"I'm fine," he said.

"You're late," said Erika.

"I know. I know. I'm sorry. I couldn't believe how long our meeting went," said Karina.

"Student Council?" I asked.

"Yeah," she said. "We're thinking of having a games week in December."

"Cool," I said. "Perhaps you could tie your week in with the Best Buddies Hooping It Up event," I said. "We talked about it in our meeting. We want to hold an event where we invite the entire school and set up hoop games around the gym. Someone suggested having a band play too and prizes."

"That's a great idea!" Karina's face lit up with enthusiasm. "We could sell drinks and snacks to make money. Thanks, Gianni. If you guys did your event on the Monday night, it could be our opening kickoff. Why don't you suggest that?"

"I'll tell Justin to talk to you." I tossed my keys back and forth in my hands. "Erika, I'm going to head out now."

"Ciao for now." She snuggled closer to her father.

Once outside, I sucked in a huge breath of fresh air as I walked to my car. I felt heavy, saddened by what I'd just seen. Erika's father was not doing well, even I could see that. I hoped that he would be able to see Erika in the play. For both of their sakes.

CHAPTER NINE
ERIKA

All day at school I was Holy Moly excited. I couldn't *fo-cus* on my work. Miss Saunders tapped her pencil on my paper and told me to concentrate. I didn't wanna listen to her. Nope, I didn't. I was going to a *re-hear-sal* to dance!

The other cast people were in the drama room when Gianni and I walked in. And that included Danny and Sandy and the Pink Ladies and all the T-birds too. Richard winked at me from across the room and that made me giggle. I think he likes me. I heard girls in the hall saying he was *hot*.

Miss Clark put us in different spots all over the room.

"Gianni," she said. "I want you and Erika to stand here."

Gianni and I moved to the place where Miss Clark told us to go. Then Amanda stood up at the front and started talking. I tried to listen. I did. I really did. But she talked fast and used words I didn't know like *ball-change*. I didn't see a ball anywhere. *Uh oh. Uh oh.* Where was the ball? I looked around the room and that made me not listen. Then I looked up at Gianni and he was listening. Then I looked around the room and everyone was staring at Amanda. When I looked at her all I could see were her lips moving and all I could hear were words jumbled together like puzzle pieces. *UH OH. UH OH. UH OH.*

"Okay," said Amanda. "I'm going to show you the first sequence. Bilal, you want to be my partner?"

Bilal went up front, and he and Amanda moved in and out and in and out. Then they twirled around.

"Everyone got it?"

"Yeah," said Gianni.

"Yup," I said but it was a lie. *Uh oh*. My mother wouldn't be happy with me.

"Let's try a count of eight," said Amanda.

Gianni took my hand in his and looked me in the eyes. "Okay, Erika. We can do this." Amanda will count to eight then we will dance for eight counts. Listen to her count, okay?"

I nodded. But my brain felt funny cuz it was all scrambled with words like *ball-change*.

Amanda counted and on eight, like Gianni said, I tried to follow him but I stepped all over his toes. *Uh oh*. I let go of his hands because they were slippery and I fell on the floor.

"Erika! Are you all right?" Gianni reached out to help me up. "I'm so sorry."

"I fell down," I said. I laughed. And I laughed and laughed. I didn't really want to laugh but I had fallen on the floor and I didn't hurt so I kept laughing.

"You sure did."

I couldn't stop laughing.

"Let's stop laughing, okay?" said Gianni.

"In *The Sound of Music* all the kids fall in the water. I'm like them."

"It's time to focus," he whispered.

I nodded. I had to *fo-cus* and listen.

"We're going to add another eight counts," said Amanda.

"Erika and Gianni, are you ready?"

"Sure are," Gianni said loudly.

By the end of the rehearsal, I was tired. My legs hurt. I was panting like a dog that had run too much. And I was sweating so it was a good thing I'd worn deodorant. I wiped the sweat from my face onto my arm.

"Maybe we should practise on our own before the next rehearsal," said Gianni. "I think that would be good for both of us."

I looked down at my feet. "My feet were slowpokes."

"We'll practise." Gianni put his hand on my shoulder. "You'll be fine."

"Gianni," said Miss Clark. "Can I talk to you and Erika for a second?" She walked over to Gianni and me.

I looked up at her and she had an even more serious look on her face than Gianni does when he's telling me something *im-port-ant*.

"I've been thinking," she said, "that maybe it would be best if Erika just did the end number." She turned to look at me. "How would you feel about that?"

I put up three fingers. "I'm in three numbers. 'Alma Mater,' 'Shakin' at the High School Hop,' and 'We Go Together.'" My name was on the list for three so that's what I wanted to do. "Three," I said.

Miss Clark put her hand on my shoulder. "I know. I understand. But… how about if we have you dance one number at the end and have you sing in the chorus for the Teen Angel number? You can wear an angel costume."

I shook my head. "Three numbers," I said, holding up three fingers again. "The *list* said so. 'Alma Mater,' 'Shakin' at the High School Hop,' and 'We Go Together.'"

Miss Clark blew air out of her mouth then looked at Gianni.

"I promise I'll help her," he said. "She can do this."

"Thank you." Miss Clark smiled at me. "Erika, you worked hard today. I know that."

After she left, Gianni put his hand on my shoulder. "Three numbers it is, kid."

"The *list* said three," I said.

"Hey, Erika!" said Sonya. She had her coat on. "You did great."

"My feet were slowpokes," I said.

"It'll just take time," she said. "You'll learn the moves. Don't give up, okay?"

"Miss Clark wants to cut her numbers," whispered Gianni to Sonya.

"I heard you," I said. Suddenly, I didn't feel very good, and my head hurt. I felt like I did when I couldn't get a problem in math or I couldn't read a big word. My feet were slowpokes, not my brain.

"Hey, some of us are going to Starbucks," said Sonya putting her arm around me. "You want to come?"

"You can get a hot chocolate," Gianni said to me.

"Starbucks! I love Starbucks."

"I'll text Karina," said Sonya, "and tell her to pick her up there instead of here."

"I can text her," I said. "From your phone."

"Sure." She played with her phone for a minute before she handed it to me. She had set it to Karina's number. I texted Karina and told her I was going to Starbucks.

As we walked out of the drama room I saw Richard. That made me smile. "I'm going to Starbucks," I said to him.

"Me too," he said. "I'll save you a seat."

"He's *hot*," I whispered to Sonya.

"One of the hottest guys at school, Erika." She raised her eyebrows up and down. Then she put her arm around me.

I said. "Are we *cel-e-brating?*"

"Sure," said Gianni. "We'll celebrate making it through our first rehearsal."

When we got to Starbucks, I ordered a hot chocolate and Gianni ordered a coffee. I wasn't allowed to drink coffee but I knew how to order my own drink. We all sat down at a big table and I sat between Gianni and Richard. He'd saved me a seat.

I licked the whipped cream off the top of my hot chocolate. Yum! One seat was open beside Gianni so when Bilal came in he sat beside him. Gianni sat up really tall and tapped his fingers on his knees. *Tap. Tap. Tap.* He just kept tapping. I don't know why he was tapping his knees like that, but he was. I liked sitting with everyone and it made me feel really good inside, like the hot chocolate did. It was *soooo* yummy. But hot. *Pfttt.* I blew on it and some of the hot chocolate spilled out so I licked the sides. Then I took little sips.

When Karina walked into Starbucks and came over to the table, I didn't want to go home.

"Time to go, Erika," said Karina, taking my coat from off my chair.

"No Way José." I held up my hot chocolate. "I'm not done."

She held up my coat. "You can take it in my car. Where's your hat?"

"In my sleeve," I said. "You know *that* cuz *that's* where it always is." I crossed my arms in front of my chest and didn't budge from my chair.

"Maybe we can rehearse later this week," said Gianni. "And go for hot chocolate again. You can have two dance rehearsals in one week if you go home with Karina now."

I thought about that before I slid off my chair. "Bye, Gianni. Bye, Richard."

Richard held up his hand and I high-fived it. Karina handed me my coat, then she picked up a serviette and wiped my face. *Yuck.* I moved my face away. I didn't like it when she did that. I wasn't a baby. I made a face at her by scrunching up my nose. She always wanted to wipe my face.

"I think I might be able to get some studio space at my dance facility." Gianni said this to Karina and not me. "I'd like to rehearse with Erika. I'll text you the reason why. I'm hoping for Saturday, and it will be in the afternoon for sure."

"Did she bomb out today?" Karina asked Gianni and not me and she lowered her voice but I still heard her.

"I can hear you!" I said, squishing my eyebrows together. I stuck out my lower lip. They were making me mad talking about me in front of me. I didn't know what *bomb out* meant but she didn't say it nicely so I didn't think it was good.

"She did fine," said Gianni. "An extra rehearsal would really help her though. The pace is fast. I'll leave it at that."

"I'll tell my mom," said Karina. "Should we be worried?"

"Not at all," said Gianni.

Karina put her hand on my shoulder. "I'm sure the extra

rehearsal will be awesome for you!"

Then Gianni nudged Sonya with his shoulder. "You want to join us?"

"Sure," she said. "I'd love to."

Karina put her hand on my back to get me to move toward the door but I turned around. I still didn't want to go with Karina.

"Erika, don't worry," said Sonya. "We can all learn the dance together."

Gianni then turned to Bilal. "You can come too, if you want. Might be great to have another couple. You know, four of us. To help Erika."

"Sure," said Bilal.

When I got home, my mom was in the kitchen stirring something. She told me she was making chili. I like chili but only if it's not too hot.

"How was your rehearsal, Erika?" she asked.

"I stepped on Gianni's toes."

"That's okay. You'll learn."

"I wanna do three numbers."

She stopped stirring and looked at me. "Why would you say that? You *are* in three numbers."

"I dunno."

My mom looked at Karina. "Do you know anything about this?"

"Let it go, Mom," said Karina. "Gianni said he'd help her. Erika got asked to go for hot chocolate with some of the cast."

"Oh, that's fun, Erika."

"I wanna take a dance class." I said loudly.

I wanted to be like Amanda and Suzanne and Claire and go to dance classes, then Miss Clark wouldn't tell me I could only do one number instead of three. I had been put on the list to dance in three numbers. I felt like my insides were steaming and bubbling and I might start yelling soon. My mom called it a meltdown.

"I think you're going to be busy, Erika," said Karina. She turned to my mother. "Mom, Gianni is going to do extra rehearsals with her."

"You're not my boss," I said, glaring at her. "Butt out."

"That's my expression," said Karina in her uppity voice.

"Erika, listen to me," said my mom. "Do you think Karina could be right?"

"She's not right." I stomped my foot and I knew my mother didn't like it when I did that.

"Er-i-ka. Are you supposed to stomp your feet?"

I frowned at my mother.

"I checked into the dance classes at the Strombie Centre for you," she said, "and on Saturday morning they have a hip hop class. You could try that."

Hip hop? Amanda and Claire didn't talk about hip hop. But I knew what hip hop was because I loved Drake and Justin Bieber.

"Justin Bieber does hip hop," I said.

"Oh for god's sake," said Karina.

"That's all they have until January," said my mother. "They said you could join even though it started a few weeks ago."

"It doesn't matter what kind of dance you do," said Karina.

"It will still help you with timing and counting and stuff."

"What if you took hip hop now," said my mother, "and then in January, after *Grease* is over, you take a jazz or tap class? I could even look into a studio for you."

I thought about this for a few seconds. I didn't like flubbing. "I want to be like Justin Bieber," I said.

"Seriously?" Karina rolled her eyes.

"Karina, that's enough," said my mother. I was glad she told uppity Karina to stop talking like that. Then my mother looked at me. "Do you want to go on Saturday? Just give it a try?"

I thought about this. "Yes," I finally said.

"She has that extra rehearsal," said Karina. "Gianni was talking about the afternoon."

"This class is in the morning." My mom looked at me. "It will be a busy day for you. Can you handle it?"

"Yes," I said.

"Okay, that's settled. I want you to feed your dad." My mom handed me a bowl of mushed-up food.

I went to the family room and my dad was sitting in his wheelchair but his head looked funny, like it was falling off his head. *Stoopid* ALS. Today he was dressed in pants and a shirt and socks and slippers. Someone always helped him get dressed. I sat on the side of the sofa that was right beside his wheelchair.

"I danced today," I said.

He tilted his head, but just a little bit. "Good."

I lifted the spoon to his mouth and he opened it. I put the food in and watched as he closed his eyes and tried to swallow. I was supposed to wait for him to let me know when he wanted more so he didn't choke. I fed him one spoonful at a time. Finally, there was one big spoonful left.

"Open up," I said.

He tried to smile at me when he opened his mouth. I put the spoon in and he sucked the food off of it. Again, I watched as he tried to swallow. This time it looked like the food was stuck. He tried and he tried to swallow. The food seemed to be caught in the middle of his throat. Then he started coughing. *Uh-oh.* My mom always patted his back when he was coughing. I went behind him and did what she did but not as hard because I couldn't hit him *that* hard. I didn't want to hurt him and hitting people wasn't nice. I patted his back over and over. He kept coughing and coughing and his back was moving up and down like he wanted to throw up. Gross. I hated throw-up. It stunk. I patted and patted his back.

"Spit," I said. That's what my mom always said if he was coughing. I leaned forward and looked at him. His face was red. It kept getting redder and redder too. "Spit," I said again.

Suddenly, my mom was running into the room so fast she knocked over a chair. She raced to my daddy and smacked his back three times, *smack, smack, smack.* I covered my ears so I couldn't hear her hand hit his back. I didn't want her to hurt him!

Food flew out of his mouth and across the room and landed on the floor in a gross clump. It looked like dog poo. Gross! I pulled my hands away from my ears and plugged my nose.

"Erika! You need to call me if he's choking!"

"I helped him," I said squeezing my hands together.

"Honey, you have to tell me if he's choking." She didn't raise her voice this time. "Call for me. It's important."

93

I felt a big lump in my throat. I had patted his back but I just couldn't hit him *hard* because hitting anyone was bad. Behind my eyes got scratchy, and then tears just ran down my face. I couldn't breathe. I gulped air. My back heaved up and down. I didn't like it when people were hit and I didn't like being yelled at. *Hiccup.* Air wouldn't go into my chest. *Hiccup.* And I didn't like it when I could only do one number and not three. *Hiccup.*

"It's not…her fault," said my dad.

"You're right," said my mother. "Erika, I'm sorry."

I looked up and I saw my mother put her face in her hands and close her eyes. "I just can't do it all," she said, and her voice sounded funny.

Karina put her hand on my mother's shoulder. "Dad, maybe it's time for a feeding tube."

He tried to nod.

My mother's shoulders started heaving up and down, like mine did when I cried, and she was breathing funny like she couldn't catch her breath. *She was crying too, like me.* She never cried. *Uh oh. Uh oh. Uh oh.* I rushed over to her and hugged her around the waist and I liked how warm her hands felt on my back.

"Don't cry," I said. "I can help. I'll make dinner two times a week." I held up two fingers.

"Oh, Erika." She stroked my hair. "You're such a love." She held me for another second then she said in a super-soft voice, "Let's sit on the sofa for a few minutes."

My mom sat at the end of the sofa beside my father's wheelchair and I sat beside my mom and Karina sat on my other side. I rested my cheek on my mom's arm. Being in the middle was good, made me feel safe.

"Let's talk...to the doctor," said my father.

"I don't know what a feeding tube is." I wiped my runny nose and leftover tears on the sleeve of my shirt.

"It's a way for Daddy to eat so he doesn't choke." First my mother pushed the hair away from my face then she turned and pushed the hair away from my father's face, and she smiled at him. "I'm glad you agree," she said to my father.

My mom put her hand on top of his. "I think we should also get a fitted neck brace for your chair."

I didn't know what a fitted brace was and I didn't want to listen to them talk.

I thought about the *tube*. All I could see in my mind was a big long hose, like a snake, that went into my father's mouth and I would have to put food in it. What if he choked when the tube was in his mouth? Suddenly my body felt cold and I wanted a warm blanket. I wouldn't like my food going through a tube to my mouth. I think that would be scary. *Uh oh. Uh oh. Uh oh.* Just seeing a funny tube in my mind made me cry again. I squeezed my eyes shut to try and get rid of the tears.

"Erika, it's okay," said Karina.

I hiccupped and it hurt. "No tube."

"The tube is something that goes directly into his stomach," said Karina. "I can show you one on the internet." She stood up and held out her hand for me to take.

I crossed my arms. "No! No tube." I shook my head.

"Erika, it'll be fine. It'll be better for Daddy," said Karina. "They just have to make a teeny-tiny cut and insert it in."

"No! No cut!"

"It's just a little cut and it will help him, Erika," said my mom. "Don't worry."

"I wanna feed him." How would I do that? I didn't want to put food into a tube that was in a cut in his stomach. Would it bleed? I didn't like blood. No! No blood. "It's my job to feed him." I said.

Karina glanced at my mother then back at me but neither of them said anything.

"How about...we find you another job?" My mother touched my arm. "Something even better."

"You can read to me," said my dad.

I shook my head, over and over, and I started to cry again, tears running down my cheeks and landing in my mouth. I spit them out because I didn't like how they tasted. Today was too many changes. Miss Clark wanted to change my dance numbers and my mother wanted to change my job. Gross, yucky, changes.

"I want a blanket," I said.

"Let's go to your room." My mother stood and reached for my hand. I held out my hand and I liked how warm hers felt in mine. Holding hands, we walked to my bedroom and I leaned my head on her arm all the way down the hall.

Before we sat on my bed she gave me Gracie, my Build-a-Bear. I'd made her at my seventh birthday party and all kinds of kids had come. In grade six, no one from my class came to my party. My mom said it was time to have family dinners for birthdays but I knew it was because the girls at school all had their own parties and I wasn't invited. Gracie had a tutu and glasses and a plaid hat that looked a lot like my hat. I hugged Gracie. Soft. She felt so soft and cuddly.

"I'm really sorry I raised my voice earlier."

"I don't like that."

"I know and I'm sorry. We all want what's best for Dad, Erika. I just had a bad moment and it wasn't right, but I was scared for him."

"I didn't want to hit him."

"I know that. I also understand this is hard for you," said my mom. "It's hard for me too and for Karina. Now I know it's been your job to feed Dad, and you've done a really good job, but if we want him to be okay, we need to have a feeding tube inserted to help him eat. Do you understand?"

I squeezed my eyes shut.

"Maybe we could think of a new job you'd like to do."

"I can make dinner two nights a week." I held up two fingers.

"That's a good one, Erika." She stroked my hair. "I bet there are other things you can do though. You like reading to him so you can continue to do that. He gets cold easily. You could put a blanket on his legs."

I thought about that.

"Okay," I said.

"That would be so good for Daddy. He'd love that. You could dance for him too."

I nodded. "I like dancing. I want to be in three numbers." I held up three fingers.

"We can talk about that later." My mom kissed my hair.

"Ok," I said. "I need a hug cuz I don't like changes."

My mother wrapped her arms around me and held me close. When she let me go she said, "Now, go give your Dad a hug too."

CHAPTER TEN
GIANNI

I took off my shoes and placed them on the shoe rack just inside the studio. Saturday afternoon at the dance studio was always pretty quiet—classes were in the morning—so the teachers were kind enough to let me have the studio space if I needed it.

I had arrived early to make sure the room was organized for our extra "Erika rehearsal," and when I got there Sonya had been sitting in her car in the parking lot, killing time.

"Amanda did a great job of the choreography," said Sonya, following me down the hall towards the back. "Although I do think the last number needs a bit of work."

"I thought that too," I said. "Something just isn't right—it's sort of, I dunno…dull. But I'm sure they'll figure it out."

We walked into the smallest of the rooms at the studio, and it was typical with mirrors at the front and a ballet bar at the back.

"What did you want to work on today?" Sonya asked as she plunked down her bag and took off her winter jacket.

"I think we should just start with the first number," I said. "Let's see how Erika does with it. It will probably be enough. I think she might have had another dance class this morning. Right now she needs repetition to get the foot speed. We can do the other numbers next time."

"Agreed," said Sonya. She went to the bar to stretch.

I walked over to the music equipment located at the side of the room.

With my back to Sonya, I fiddled around with the buttons, turning everything on. By now, I had all the songs from the musical on my phone so I plugged it in and set it up. I scrolled through my playlist.

I suddenly could smell freshness and flowers with a hint of vanilla and spice. Sonya must have floated across the floor. Seriously. I didn't hear her. She snuggled her arms around my waist, clasping her hands in front of me and leaning her cheek against my back. Her breasts too. Her body breathed against mine, inhaling in, exhaling out, almost as if we were an instrument. I waited for something to happen, for me to feel something like tingles, shivers or sensations in the places I should feel sensations.

Anything.

Nothing.

She felt comfortable like a favourite blanket, secure and friendly and, well, like Sonya, my best friend. But that was it.

I touched her hands, wanting to unclasp them so I could move away from her but she had me in a tight hold. I knew I should lean back against her, moan, groan, tell her how good she felt but I couldn't. It would be a lie. I had no idea how to get out of this embrace without hurting her.

Maybe this was a sign. An opportunity. Maybe Sonya could be the first person I told…

I hesitated, and the sound of familiar footsteps in the hall outside the room saved me from making a decision.

"Here comes Erika." I unleashed myself from her grasp.

But not before Sonya had managed to kiss the side of my neck. The wetness of saliva rested on my skin, and when she turned to greet Erika, I instinctively tried to wipe it off. Sonya caught my gesture in the mirror and I saw her shoulders sag.

But only for a second.

Erika ran over to Sonya and gave her a hug.

"We're going to have fun today," said Sonya, hugging her back, her back now straight as a board.

"I went to hip hop," said Erika, all smiles.

"Show us what you learned," said Sonya.

"You get down and *funky*," said Erika, doing a hip hop arm movement. Sonya and I laughed and the tension seemed to be broken, a little anyway.

Erika performed a few hip hop moves for us and both Sonya and I joined in, all three of us facing the mirror. Bilal walked in and stared at us, and just like that, my heart sped up and my nerves seemed to go wacky on me, but in a good way. And yes, without even touching him, I felt tingles.

"Whoa," he said.

After a few more minutes of horsing around, I went back to the music equipment and started playing the first song.

"Do you remember some of the moves we learned for this one?" I asked Erika.

"*Yeeees.*" She hid behind her hands. "I stepped on your toes."

"That's over," said Sonya. "That's why we're here today."

"Maybe Bilal and Sonya can show you the moves," I said.

I played the music while Bilal and Sonya danced. Although he wasn't a dancer, Bilal had a natural rhythm that made his body just seamlessly flow from one move to the next.

His feet and hips pivoted perfectly and his upper torso looked lean and strong. He was most definitely in total control, guiding and gliding Sonya through each move. I wished I was the one he was guiding, that his hand was on my back.

When they finished, Erika clapped and I shook my head slightly to clear it.

"Now it's our turn," I said. "But why don't we start with one count of eight."

Bit by bit, we worked on each eight count, and once Erika had the sequence figured out, we strung two together, then three, then four until she had learned most of the song.

One quick glance at the clock and I realized we'd been rehearsing for an hour. Sweat glistened on Erika's forehead.

"I'm pooped," said Erika, flopping on the floor.

"I think we're done for today," I said.

"That was awesome," said Bilal. His cheeks were a bit flushed. A few locks of his hair were streaked with sweat and hung haphazardly across his forehead. "You helped me too, Erika." He sat down beside her. "I'll let you in on a secret."

"I don't like secrets."

"Me neither," said Bilal. He nudged his shoulder against hers in a friendly gesture. "I'll just tell you something then and it won't be a secret." He nudged her shoulder again. "I stepped on my partner's toes too when we danced in rehearsal."

"I *crunched* Gianni's toes," said Erika. "And I fell down."

"That's okay," he said. "No one's perfect." Bilal's low voice seemed to get under my skin and into my blood, making it rush through my body and my head, making me almost dizzy.

Sonya picked up her bag from the floor. "We should get going, Erika."

"You're driving her?" I asked.

Sonya nodded but avoided looking at me. "I told her mother I'd bring her home. Karina had something to do." She put her hand out for Erika to grab. "Let's go, girl."

While Erika got her coat and hat on, and ate one of Sonya's granola bars, I went over to the music equipment and turned everything off, keeping an eye on Bilal in the mirror, as he gathered his things and also put on his coat. Maybe we could go for coffee?

Sonya adjusted Erika's hat. "We're heading out," said Sonya.

"Me too," said Bilal.

We all walked down the hall together but when we got to the door, Bilal stopped and searched his pockets. "I think I forgot my keys," he said. "I'll be right back."

"I'll wait," I said.

"We'll go," said Sonya.

Erika hugged me. "You're the bestest Best Buddy ever."

"Aww," I said. "Likewise." I winked at her. "You were amazing today. Miss Clark is going to be happy."

Erika put three fingers up. "Three dances."

"Okay, star," said Sonya. "We need to get a move on." She opened the studio door and ushered Erika outside. The snow had stopped. Only a light skiff sat on the ground.

"Bye, Gianni," said Erika.

"Bye," I said back.

Not a word from Sonya.

When Bilal came back around the corner, Erika and Sonya were gone. "Find your keys?" I asked Bilal.

"Yeah, they were on the floor. You forgot this." He handed me my scarf.

"Hey, thanks." I took it from him and when I did, our hands touched. Shivers coursed through me.

Our eyes met. I held his gaze. I swear if I'd had the guts I could/would/might've kissed him. Or maybe not.

Bilal opened the door. The brisk winter air felt amazing and I gulped in a breath, trying to calm down. I wanted to ask him to go for coffee but my throat had gone totally dry.

Do it now, I thought.

"Youuhwanttogoforcoffee?" I asked. Awkward.

Bilal glanced at his watch. "My bus will be here in ten minutes."

"I can drive you," I said.

He shrugged. "Sure. My studying can wait."

"What are you working on?"

We talked school all the way to the coffee shop, which worked for me because it was generic and easy and our conversation went back and forth. Both of us were taking a full load of sciences and found physics harder than biology and math, and chemistry was a so-so, not easy but not too demanding. I liked English, he didn't. Drama, for both of us, was an easy credit but he was in *Grease* hoping to bump up his drama mark to ultimately bump up his GPA. I asked him about the soccer team and he told me about how awesome Richard was, and a jealous jab smacked me in the stomach.

"Why did Richard audition for *Grease*?" I asked. "He's not in drama."

"The challenge. He's just that kind of guy."

Richard likes the girls, I told myself as we entered the coffee shop.

"What are you getting to drink?" I asked him in the line-up.

So far we hadn't come close to touching but I wanted to, so I leaned into him a little when I talked.

"Mocha," he replied. "You?" He didn't move away.

Had he felt my breath on his neck? "Straight java," I said.

We got our drinks and he paid for both of ours with a Starbucks card. "Payment for the ride home," he insisted.

We found a seat in the corner and for a few seconds we sipped our drinks without talking. Had we used up our conversation already?

"Erika did great today," he said.

"She'll catch on." I played with my paper cup, twirling it around. "She just needs time. Like all of us at different things. Me in math."

"Me in English." he laughed.

"But not soccer," I said.

"Yeah, but soccer and English aren't exactly in the same 'fun' categories."

"At our last Best Buddies meeting, we talked about having a Hooping It Up event. You should get your soccer team out. Maybe we can set up a few competitions, like the soccer team against the volleyball team."

"We'd kick their butts." He laughed again. Then he leaned back, flicking his bangs back with his fingers.

We chatted on about the Hooping It Up event, and he had some great suggestions about how we could make it better. I was going to talk to Justin for sure about some of Bilal's ideas. All too soon, for me anyway, our drinks were finished and we were standing to leave.

His glove dropped and I immediately bent over to pick it up but so did he and our hands touched, for a brief second.

Then he grabbed his glove and stood, glancing around the coffee shop, shifty-eyed almost.

We didn't say much to each other in the car. There was a sort of awkwardness looming over us now as I drove. I stared straight ahead, and he sat in the passenger seat but he only spoke to give me directions to his house. After weaving through a few suburban streets, I finally was in front of his small brick house. It hit me that I knew very little about him, except he was Lebanese, played soccer, liked singing, and drank mochas.

"Thanks," he said, sitting in the car but not making a move to get out.

"No problem," I said. "I might be taking Erika bowling next weekend." I continued talking and I hoped I wasn't coming across like I was babbling. "You should join us. It would be a good intro for you for Best Buddies. They'll be looking for new people to join."

He slowly turned, staring me directly in the eyes. I didn't divert my gaze but stared deep into his. My heart pounded through my clothes in anticipation.

"That sounds good," he said, breaking our spell.

I let out a loud exhale, totally unaware that I'd been holding my breath. And then, he jumped out of the car and made a bee-line to his front door, his head ducked into his coat like a three-banded armadillo curling into its shell. Shocked at his abrupt departure, I watched him leave. I had to. Watch. Every. Move.

Once he was in the house, and the door was shut, I sped away from the curb, my hands shaking, my body vibrating, and my pulse racing.

What had just happened? Had it just happened? My first

real connect? Or was I concocting everything in my mind to make it be the way I wanted it to be? No! I had felt the intensity, the passion, the excitement of possibly being kissed. I had felt it! It was real.

I arrived home and breathed a sigh of relief that no one was in the kitchen. I grabbed a glass of water and a bag of chips and made my way downstairs. At the bottom, I heard Rob clicking away on his computer, rap music playing in the background. Instead of passing his room, I knocked on the door.

"Yo," he said.

"Whatcha doing?" I asked, pushing his door open.

"Stupid homework. Mid-terms." He leaned back in his chair and crossed his arms across his chest, tapping his hands under his pits. He stared at me. "Where were you?"

"Extra rehearsal for the musical."

"Oh, so that's why you look like you just ran a marathon."

I touched my cheek, and sure enough, it still felt hot. Not from rehearsal, though. As I plopped down on the end of his bed, it occurred to me that if I was going to talk to anyone, Rob should be the one. *Could I?* We'd always been close even though we were completely different. In high school Rob had been the school hot-guy, the one the girls threw themselves at. My mother always complained she couldn't keep up with the names of his girlfriends, so she called each girl Stella, which, of course, embarrassed Rob and made him go ballistic on her. Mom and I got along: Rob and her not so much.

Still, I knew Rob wouldn't judge me.

How could I tell him? Should I tell him? After what had happened with Bilal, I was convinced I knew what I'd known since extra hair had arrived on my body when I was thirteen.

*No. Stick with **the plan.***

"How's school for you?" He broke into the dialogue going on in my head. "Dad still nagging you to go into engineering?"

"Yeah," I said. "He's obsessed. I've got another year after this one to decide. I haven't figured anything out yet."

"You just have to stand up to him."

"He'll be paying the bills."

"Yeah, ain't that the truth. And he'll let you know it too."

"I didn't get the lead in *Grease*," I mumbled. "That news won't help my cause if I decide to take theatre arts instead of engineering."

"Really? That sucks. Who did?"

"Richard Temple."

"The soccer star? Can he sing?"

"A little. Probably enough to get through."

"Who are you?"

"Eugene." I stared at the checkered pattern on his comforter.

"No way!"

I looked up and shook my head as I blew out a huge breath of air. "Yes, way. They screwed me."

"No kidding. But, hey, Eugene is hilarious. You could make him huge."

I glanced up and managed a half-decent smile. "I plan to. Don't worry, I'll make people laugh."

"Yeah, you will, little brother. You're crazy talented."

I broke out laughing and tossed a pillow at his head. "Yeah, I'm crazy all right."

He caught it mid-air and chucked it back at me from behind his back. I caught it and threw it at the toy basketball hoop he still had screwed into his wall. He'd put it there when he was twelve and I was nine. We used to sit on his bed and throw socks into it, playing 21.

"You look like you got the world on your skinny shoulders."

"I kinda do," I said without thinking.

"What's up?" He leaned back in his chair. "Talk to me."

I stared, fixated on the little chips of paint on the rim of the basketball hoop. "I think…"

Just say it. SAY IT!

"I think I might be gay," I blurted out.

"No shit, Sherlock," he said.

My head jerked up and I stared at him with my mouth wide open. "What?"

"I coulda told you that years ago."

"I wear normal clothes. Jeans. Hoodies."

"It doesn't matter what you wear, Bro. You've always been different. For one thing, you don't like girls. I'd point out a girl with a good rack and you'd look dazed and confused."

"So, that obvious?"

"Yes…and no." He ducked his head, looking a bit sheepish.

"What's that supposed to mean?"

"Weeeell, remember the time I borrowed your computer?" He made a little grimace. "I saw that you'd logged on to some sites where they answer questions about being gay. You had Googled, 'how do you know?' and 'what are the signs?' It all made sense to me then. Your lack of liking *girls*. When I was your age I was Googling 'hot girls.'"

"I looked at those sites because…because I was trying to figure it out, I guess. I don't want anyone else to know, okay?"

He shrugged. "It's your business."

"Mom and Dad will freak."

"Nah, I don't think so. But tell them when you're ready. It's your call."

"I think…I want to wait to get out of high school before I really come out." I paused for a second and thought about what I had just said. "I can't believe I just said that. *Coming out.* It's so weird to say it out loud." I paused for a split second. "Don't tell anyone," I repeated.

"You are who you are, that's it, that's all. Hey, it's not like it used to be. I have friends who aren't gay and they've joined the Pride Club at university. It's becoming kind of normal. Not a big deal."

I thought about the guys circling me in the parking lot. "I'm not so sure about that," I said quietly.

His eyes narrowed into slits. "Someone harassing you?"

Rob had always had my back and I could see by the look in his eyes that wasn't going to change. But if he did something, made a racket with those idiots, I would lose because everyone would find out and I didn't want that. Not yet. Plus, since I'd changed my parking spot they weren't bugging me at all. In fact, they'd passed me in the hall at school today and not a word.

"Nothing I can't handle right now," I said.

"Okay. But you let me know if anyone bothers you."

"Thanks." I sighed again. This was complicated.

"So…you haven't told anyone else? I'm seriously the only one?"

"You're it." I paused before I said, "Sonya made a pass at me today."

"Damn. She's hot. What a waste!"

"Dude, that's just creepy. She's in my grade."

"You're right. A bit young for me." He paused and the expression on his face turned serious. "When you finally come out to everyone, are you going to do that whole Gay Pride deal? Am I gonna have to walk to support you?"

I shrugged. "I haven't really thought about it. I don't think it's really me either, but who knows?"

"Well, I guess I'd walk for you. If you wanted me to."

"You'd do that for me?"

"Of course." He paused before he grinned. "But can you see Dad out there?"

I laughed for a few seconds before I sobered up. "I don't want to tell them."

"Don't worry about Mom and Dad. I think they'll be just fine. Mom for sure. And Dad, well, he'll get over it. And the twins are too stupid to know anything."

And then in typical Rob fashion his expression changed and he grinned from ear to ear. "Now Nonna, she might be another issue. She's the one you have to worry about. She might run you over with her walker."

"Nonna! Oh, crap, I forgot about her." I rolled back on the bed, laughing. Just talking to Rob made me feel as if a twenty-pound weight had been removed from my shoulders.

One down. And I felt good, relieved, and I didn't feel that horrible. It had been okay.

CHAPTER ELEVEN
ERIKA

I heard the hip hop music before I even entered the room. Holy Moly, I liked it. It was *chill*. I was gonna *rock* it.

"Sounds like fun," said Karina. She was taking me to my hip hop class.

"I'm gonna *rock it*," I said out loud. "My teacher's name is Corey Borg."

When I entered the room, I saw Jimmy, dressed in shorts and running shoes and a t-shirt. "How come you're here?" He asked as he pushed his glasses up his nose. "You weren't here last time."

"I want to take dance classes cuz I'm in three numbers in the musical *Grease* at our school." I held up my fingers and showed him the number three. "'Alma Mater,' 'Shakin' at the High School Hop,' and 'We Go Together.' You should come watch."

"I'm on it!" Jimmy held up his thumb.

"Okay, everyone!" The teacher turned down the music before he spoke from the front of the room. He wore long yellow shorts, shoes like Justin Bieber wore, and a red shirt. What I liked best was the cloth wrapped around his forehead.

"Find a spot that is not too close to your neighbour," he said. "Put out your arms and make sure you can't touch." He stood with his arms out, looking like a letter T.

I stood beside Jimmy and held out my arms. He held out his too. We didn't touch so we didn't have to move. No Siree.

"Okay, it looks great," said the teacher. "Before we start I want to welcome Erika. She's new to our class today." He waved to me. "Hi, Erika. My name is Corey."

I waved back. "I'm gonna *rock it* today."

"That's the spirit," said Corey. "Because Erika is new, I'm going to go over a few of the moves we did last week. Erika, you'll have to listen carefully. Everyone has to get down and get funky, okay?"

"*Funky,*" I said.

Corey explained eight counts without the music. I liked the moves. They were different than the ones we did at rehearsal for *Grease* and they were *funky*. We went over them four times without any music.

Then he put the music on and I liked hip hop music. The dance moves seemed easier than *Grease* and I learned I could do them even though I'd missed the first class. All class we did eight counts without the music then eight counts with the music and we kept doing more eight counts. And I was good. Really good. Jimmy kept flubbing and laughing. He was better at running. Yup. He was.

When the class ended Corey came up to me and said, "You did fantastic, Erika. Wow, I'm impressed."

I looked up at him and held up three fingers. "I'm in three numbers in *Grease* at my school. 'Alma Mater,' 'Shakin' at the High School Hop,' and 'We Go Together.' I get to wear a poodle skirt." I stared at his hair. "What are you wearing on your head?"

Corey touched the red cloth thing. "This?"

"I like it."

"It's a bandana."

"I want one. You can come to *Grease*. The tickets cost fifteen dollars."

Corey smiled at me and held up his thumb. "I can handle that."

Jimmy's mom and my mom were waiting for us at the door of the dance room.

"How was your class?" my mom asked. "You look like you worked hard."

"*Funky*," I said. "And I didn't say the F-word. I said *Funky*."

"Let's see what you learned at your hip hop class this morning," said Sonya at Gianni's dance studio after I had hugged her.

Gianni and Sonya lined up in front of the mirror with me and I showed them all the new moves I'd learned and I remembered all of them.

Then Bilal showed up and we danced for one whole hour and by the time we were finished I was sweating a lot, like all over my forehead and above my lip and on my back. Holy Moly, I was pooped. I plopped down on the floor.

"You did awesome," said Sonya. "Do you need some water?"

"Yes, please."

"And I have a granola bar in my backpack. Do you want it?"

Dancing so much did make me really hungry and really, really thirsty. "Yes, please."

My mom had told me Sonya was driving me home. After

I drank some water and ate her granola bar, she helped me up because I was too tired to get up by myself. My legs felt like rubber bands. I bet when I got home I could eat a whole box of mac and cheese all by myself. Yum! Tonight *I* was making mac and cheese from the box. What a busy day! Holy Moly. I wanted to go home and see my dad but I wasn't allowed to feed him anymore even though he didn't have a feeding tube yet.

When Sonya and I were at the front door of the dance studio, I said goodbye to Gianni, but Sonya didn't say goodbye at all. I frowned. I thought she liked him? My mom told me it was polite to say goodbye and to say it properly but sometimes I liked to say *Ciao for now*.

Outside the snow had stopped falling from the sky but the sidewalks were slippery. Sonya linked her arm in mine and we walked all the way to her car together. I got in Sonya's car and buckled up my seatbelt. When she was buckled up and driving I said, "You didn't say bye to Gianni."

"Yes, I did," she said.

"No Way José."

"Okay, so I forgot."

"You don't like him anymore?"

"I like him, Erika. But we're just friends. Like you and I are friends."

"Not like Karina and Cameron are friends?"

"No. Not like that."

Sonya looked straight ahead. To me she looked really sad because she wasn't smiling not even a little bit. "I wish you and Gianni were like Karina and Cameron," I said. "Cuz you're both my best friends."

"Me too," she said. "But I think Gianni just wants us to be

friends." Then she pointed out the window. "Oh, look, Erika. The sun is peeking out from under that cloud. I love it when the sun shines." She sighed a little bit. "It's supposed to really snow on Monday."

"Maybe I can make snow angels," I said. "I *loooove* making snow angels."

On Monday morning, I woke up and my Groovy Groove was not the same. My mom forgot to play my knock-knock joke so I didn't get out of bed. Then she came in and had to make me get out of bed. And I stomped across the hall.

After my time in the bathroom, I went back to my room and shut my door. Sometimes if I just talked about things all by myself everything got better in my brain. I sat on my bed and held Gracie and rocked back and forth.

"My daddy is going to the hospital today. I don't think I like hospitals. But he needs to get something put in his stomach so he doesn't choke. I don't like it when he chokes. I hope he doesn't die. I want him to be okay and come and see me sing and dance. I've never been to a hospital before. They scare me."

Someone knocked on my door. "Erika?" It was my mom. "Your breakfast is ready. Daddy wants to say goodbye to you before we go."

I thought about that. If I didn't say goodbye then my Groove was really all mixed up. I couldn't answer my mom cuz I was thinking.

My mother opened my door a little and looked at me. "Don't you want to say goodbye to Daddy? It's your last chance."

I put Gracie back on my pillow and stood up.

My mother walked into my room and hugged me. "It is going to be okay."

I didn't answer her but after she left I got dressed and went to the kitchen. Everything was all mixed up because my father was dressed and sitting in his wheelchair. I went over to him and held his hand.

He tried to reach up but he couldn't, so I leaned over so he could touch my cheek.

"I saw the tube," I said to him. Karina had shown me a picture of the feeding tube my dad was getting on the computer. I didn't want that funny thing in my dad's stomach.

"It's going to be a good thing," he said.

My mother touched my shoulder. "It's time to eat your breakfast. Daddy and I have to leave soon because we need to be at the hospital by eight."

Tears sprang out from behind my eyes. Words were in my brain but I didn't know how to get them out. Sometimes they wouldn't come out of my mouth because they had to stay inside first. I had to think about them.

"This will be good for Daddy." My mom hugged me. "He won't choke anymore."

I sniffled and wrapped my arms around her. She patted my back a few times before she let me go to sit my special chair. "Would you like to eat your Cheerios without milk this morning?"

I nodded. Then I thought of something. "Excuse me," I said.

I ran from the room, got the blanket off the sofa, and brought it back to my dad. I put the blanket on his legs.

"Thank you," he said.

I sat down to eat my breakfast.

"This is just a routine procedure," said my mom.

I looked up at her. I didn't know what *routine pro-ced-ure* meant. "Knock, knock," I said.

She gave me a little smile. "Who's there?"

"Orange?"

"Orange who?"

"Orange you glad you didn't say banana?"

My mother tried to laugh but it didn't come out very well. I didn't laugh either.

Karina didn't put the timer on me because she had to help my mom get my dad in the van. Antonio was meeting my mom at the hospital. I don't think I like hospitals. My dad has a ramp outside for his wheelchair. When Karina came back in, she was covered in snow and looked like she had white hair.

"I hope it doesn't snow too much," she said. Her voice sounded funny and not like morning-bossy Karina.

I glanced up from my plate and stared at her face. "I don't want Daddy to go to the hospital."

"I don't either." She picked up her smoothie glass and even though it was still full she dumped it down the sink.

"You didn't finish," I said.

"I'm not hungry." She clicked the timer around. "Five minutes, okay? I want to leave a little early because of the snow."

"Erika, what's the matter?" Miss Saunders was already at my locker. I knew I was being a slowpoke but my heart felt heavy, like it was also wearing big winter boots.

"My dad had to go to the hospital."

Her eyes widened. "Oh no. Is he okay?"

"He's gotta get a feeding tube."

"Oh, Erika, I'm so sorry. Will he be in the hospital long?"

"I dunno." In my mind I could see blood spurting from my dad's tummy. I shivered, like I was outside without my coat on and it was snowing and snowing. "I don't like blood."

Miss Saunders wrapped her arms around me. "Let's go to science and forget about this for a little while."

School seemed to go by so slowly and all I could think of was my dad so I didn't *fo-cus* at all. NO. I didn't.

After school, Gianni met me at the locker and we walked to the drama room.

"My dad had to go to the hospital today," I said.

"Are you okay?" He put his arm around me.

All day in my mind, I'd seen blood coming out of his tummy. My teachers said it was okay that I wasn't listening and they said they understood how sad I was.

We walked down the hall without talking cuz it was too hard for me to talk and think and walk.

At the drama room door, Gianni said, "Let's focus on the rehearsal, okay? It could take your mind off your father. You did awesome on Saturday."

"I want to do good today," I said. "But I'm sad."

"I understand."

Rehearsal started right away. Gianni always said Miss Clark was *no nonsense.*

"Okay, everyone," she said. "We are going to review the first song. Then I'd like to go through the choreography for 'Shakin' at the Hop.' At least the first half."

When the music went on, Gianni smiled at me. "Think about the music," he whispered.

He took my hand and we danced like we had on Saturday. "You're doing fabulous!" he said when he had pulled me in, just before I was to move out.

As I danced, my heart started to feel better, lighter and lighter, and my feet moved like they were supposed to and I never once stepped on Gianni's toes or fell down. When the song was over, Gianni held his thumbs up.

"Nice work, everyone." Miss Clark clapped her hands and looked over at me and Gianni. "Erika, that was fantastic."

Gianni held up his hand and I high-fived it.

"I think it needs a few tweaks," said Miss Clark. "Well a lot of tweaks, but we'll leave it for today. Let's move on. If we can get the music done, then we can add the blocking you've been doing with Mr. Warner."

Miss Clark called Amanda and Suzanne up to the front. I tried to listen to them talk about the next song but the words got all jumbled in my brain. All I could see was my father, and his tummy had a cut and blood. I couldn't remember one move when the music went on.

"I can't," I said.

"Shhh." Gianni put his finger to his mouth. "Don't say that," he whispered. "I will practise with you again."

I lowered my head. "I can't *fo-cus* today. My dad's in the hospital."

"I will talk to Miss Clark," said Gianni.

Gianni talked to Miss Clark. Miss Clark, like all my other teachers, understood that I was sad. She let me step on Gianni's toes and didn't tell me that I couldn't be in three numbers.

After the rehearsal, when we were getting our winter coats on, Gianni's phone beeped. He looked at it.

"Erika," he said. "Karina was running errands in her spare but the roads are bad, so she wants to go straight to the hospital."

"Oh no, oh no, oh no," I said. Suddenly my tummy felt sick and my head didn't feel so good either.

"Don't worry. I'll drive you," said Gianni. "Karina wants me to take you to the hospital because it's on my way home and your mom is still there." He lifted my chin. "You'll get to see your dad."

Inside I started to shake. I didn't want to go to the hospital. Nope. I didn't.

I shook my head. "No hospital."

"Just think, you can give him a hug. He'd like that."

I thought about this for a second. "Okay."

Gianni was helping me put on my coat when Bilal walked over to talk to him and me too. "Are we still going bowling this week sometime?" He asked winking at me.

"My dad's in the hospital."

"I'm sorry. I hope he's okay," said Bilal.

I looked around the room to see if I could see Sonya but she was busy talking to Amanda and Claire.

"Is Sonya coming bowling too?" I asked.

"She could," said Bilal.

"Probably not," said Gianni.

The snow on the ground made it look like a big white pillow. It wasn't snowing anymore though and the sky was almost dark. When I walked to Gianni's car, the snow was almost as high as my winter boots. Gianni didn't park in his usual spot. His car was behind the big blue garbage. I did up my seatbelt while Gianni used a long brush to clean off his windshield. *Sweep. Sweep.* Back and forth. Before he got in the car, he shook out his hair and brushed off his shoulders. Warm air was coming through the little vents by the time he got in the car.

He started to back his car up but it went *clunk, clunk, clunk.*

"What the heck?" Gianni put on his brakes and stopped his car.

Gianni opened his car door and stepped outside. The cold air swirled in so I huddled into my winter coat like a turtle. Gianni shut the door and warm air flowed through the little vents again. I watched Gianni walk around his car but when he got to the front he glanced down.

"No way!" he yelled. I heard him even though I was inside the car and he was outside.

He pulled his phone out of his pocket. Who was he calling? I wasn't sure until he said, "Hey, Sonya."

I liked that he was calling Sonya.

He walked back and forth in front of the car and I couldn't hear what he was saying to Sonya. Then Gianni opened his door and the cold air blasted into the car again.

"Erika," he said as he got in the car. "I've got a flat." He shut his car door and I was glad cuz I was freezing.

"Sonya is going to come and take you to the hospital, okay?" He rubbed his hands together. "I can't believe this," he muttered.

I knew what a flat tire was. Yup, I did. It was when the tire lost all its air. Once I was with my dad, when I was ten years old, and we were driving down the road and his car did the same thing. It went *clunk, clunk, clunk.* So he pulled off to the side of the road and got something out of the trunk called a jack and he pressed it up and down and up and down and lifted the car right off the ground.

"My dad got a flat in summer, not winter."

"I wish it was summer," said Gianni. He leaned over and opened up his glove compartment and pulled out gloves. "I think I'm going to need these."

Out the window, I saw Sonya coming toward the car. She opened my door. "Come on, you," she said to me. "I'll take you to see your dad."

"Thanks again," said Gianni to Sonya.

"Of course," she said. "It sucks. That you have a flat, I mean."

"Sucks isn't a strong enough word," said Gianni.

"What are you going to do?" She asked.

"Change it."

"You want me to help you? My dad forced me to practise before I got my licence. Erika could sit in my car for a few minutes."

I felt like my head was at a ping pong game as I turned from Gianni to Sonya to Gianni to Sonya. Back and forth. We had a ping pong table in our backyard and Karina and her friends played all the time and I played sometimes too. My dad would hit the ball to me but mostly I missed and had to run to pick it up. He and Karina would go back and forth but now he can't do that. He told me his muscles are being stubborn like I am sometimes when I just say NO.

"It's okay," said Gianni. "It's more important for you to get Erika to the hospital."

"I wish you weren't such a nice guy." Sonya held out her hand for me. "Come on, let's get you to see your dad."

Sonya drove slowly, like really slowly, but I didn't mind. I didn't want to get in an accident. Finally, she pulled into a parking spot by a huge building, with a lot of windows and a lot of floors.

"We're here," she said.

I stared and stared at the big building.

"Are you okay?" she asked.

"I dunno."

"Karina told me what floor and room," said Sonya. "I'll walk you up."

"I need to think," I said.

"Sure."

We sat in the car and just sat there. I didn't want to go in the hospital but I wanted to see my dad.

Finally, I said, "Okay."

"I'll go with you," she said.

Once she had bought a parking ticket, we walked through doors that automatically opened. Then we headed down a long, long hall. The hospital smelled funny, and I didn't like it very much. Yuck. It made my nose itchy. Then I plugged my nose. "It stinks."

"All hospitals smell the same," said Sonya. "Antiseptic."

"I don't know that word."

"It's stuff to make it sterile so it has no germs."

We walked down two long halls before we got in an elevator. Sonya pressed number 4. I watched the numbers go by as we went up the elevator. As soon as we were out, Sonya looked at all the signs before she pointed and said, "This way."

We stopped at a door that was half open and I saw my dad lying on the hospital bed. At first I just stood there and didn't want to go in. What if he was bleeding? I looked at the sheets but didn't see any blood. No. I didn't see blood.

"Erika!" I turned to see my mother walking toward me and she was holding a coffee. "Thank you so much for bringing her, Sonya."

"No problem," said Sonya. "You know I'd do anything for her. How are *you* doing?"

"Hanging in there." My mother held up her coffee. "Thanks for asking. I'll be better with caffeine."

"I should get going." Sonya put her hand on my shoulder. "Have a good visit with your dad, okay? You did a great job tonight at rehearsal."

I hugged Sonya. "Thank you for the ride."

"You're welcome."

After she left my mother took my hand. "Come on. Let's go see Daddy. He's doing great."

But my feet wouldn't move.

"Do you think Daddy wants to see you?" my mother asked.

I nodded.

"I think so too," she said.

We walked into the room to see my dad who had his eyes open and didn't look any sicker than he did when he left in the morning. "Do you have that tube now?"

"Yes."

"Does it hurt?"

"No."

"I don't want you to hurt."

"How was school?" he asked.

"I didn't do much cuz my brain kept thinking that you might be bleeding."

"Don't worry." He closed his eyes.

I pushed his hair off his forehead just like my mother did. "You're going to get better, Daddy."

"Oh, Erika." He opened his eyes and looked at me.

Although my dad's body had changed and how he talked had changed, his eyes were still the same and I knew how he felt just by looking into his eyes.

"Don't be sad," I said.

"I'm sorry."

"It's okay."

"It's not." He blinked and tears rolled down his cheek.

"Stoopid ALS," I said.

One side of his mouth lifted in a little smile. "So smart. Stupid ALS."

"I know I'm smart," I said. "Cuz all my life you've told me that."

CHAPTER TWELVE
GIANNI

Frozen fingers made me curse under my breath. I stopped trying to get the jack up, peeled off my useless glove and blew on my fingers to thaw them out. Why tonight of all nights? Here I thought I was safe by the garbage dumpster. What an idiot I was. Exactly where you'd expect to find broken glass.

"Do you need help?" I looked up to see Anna and Justin standing beside me.

"Sure," I said without hesitation.

With Justin's help, we had the car propped up in no time, but taking off the nuts was a lot harder to do in the cold. We had the wrench that fit them perfectly but they weren't budging.

"Maybe if we both haul on it," said Justin.

Both of us grabbed on to the wrench and I could feel his breath on my face and the close proximity of his body. We pushed down on the wrench and with a bit of tugging one of the nuts loosened.

"That's one," he said.

The rest came off a little easier. Once they were off, I yanked on the tire until it was lying in the snow. Then Justin handed me the donut and I put it on.

"I think I can finish," I said, standing and shaking my head to get the snow off my hair.

"Yeah, they go on easier than they come off," said Justin.

"Thanks, again," I said.

Anna peeked out from under her scarf, something I wished I had. "I heard Erika's dad had to go into the hospital," she said.

"He needed a feeding tube," I replied.

Justin blew on his hands before he shoved them in his pockets. "Is he doing okay?"

"It's hard to tell," I said. "It all started off in his thumbs, I know that. But it seems to have affected his esophagus."

Anna nodded thoughtfully. A med school wanna-be, she was a science genius. "It's a disease that hits everyone differently," she said.

"How's Erika doing?" Justin asked.

"It's tough. She likes routine and structure."

Anna linked her arm in Justin's. "Let us know if we can be of any help."

I nodded. "Thanks. Good thing she's got *Grease* and the Hooping It Up event."

"Oh, hey, thanks for talking to Bilal," said Justin. "We've got the soccer team playing the volleyball team. It should be a blast."

"Great," I said. "So, is Willa's band playing?" I asked with a bit of a smirk.

"Oh, yeah," said Anna. "She should be in sales."

"Hey, what's going on here?" A voice sounded from behind me and it made my heart pick up its pace. Bilal appeared from somewhere, and heat flushed my cheeks as my blood ran hot, making me forget about being cold.

"Hey, Bilal," said Justin. They slapped hands like two buddies meeting on the golf course.

"We gotta go, Justin," said Anna. "I'm freezing. This snow is not my thing." She lifted her foot to show a flat shoe and no socks. "My footwear needs revamping."

"I'm good here," I said, waving for both of them to leave. "Thanks again for your help."

Once Justin and Anna were gone, Bilal pointed to the tire. "Sucks to have your luck."

"Yeah, I know. Oh well. I just have to put the nuts back on."

"I can help," said Bilal. "Give me the flat and I'll shove it in the trunk."

We finished up and I slapped my hands together.

"Want a ride home?" I asked. "Least I can do."

"This is getting to be a habit," he said.

Yeah, and one I really like, I thought.

Once inside the car, I got the heater on but it blew cold air. I backed up, slowly, driving like an old grandmother. The donut tire combined with snow didn't give me a ton of confidence.

"The choreography is coming along," I said, clenching the steering wheel until my hands ached.

"It's decent," said Bilal. "Amanda and Claire have done an amazing job. And I have to admit—Richard and Sonya are good as Danny and Sandy. They work."

"Yeah, Richard has shown up to play. He's seriously working on being Zuko."

"You were hilarious in the last acting rehearsal." Bilal laughed. "You're taking Eugene to the next level."

"Thanks." His compliment made my cheeks heat up. Again. "He's a better character than I first thought. I'm definitely okay with him."

Up ahead was a red light so I braked, which sent my car sliding and my heart catapulting. I quickly pumped the brakes and fortunately no one was in front of me or beside me. I swerved a bit, righted the car, and managed to stop it before the crosswalk.

"Wow, it's slippery." My entire body trembled and my heart pounded.

"Good driving," said Bilal, putting a gentle hand on my shoulder. My heart slowed and all that pent up driving stress seemed to melt away at his touch.

I glanced at him and we locked eyes and I swear something was there, I could see it.

We are alike, I thought.

A horn sounded behind me and when I looked up, the light was green.

I made it to Bilal's house and parked in front. We sat there for a few moments and when I couldn't stand the electrical tension anymore I reached across and put my hand on his in a bold move. "Thanks for your help," I said softly.

He didn't move his hand and instead interlaced his fingers through mine. We sat there for a few seconds not talking and the car took on a weird silence, which, of course, wasn't really silent. I could hear heat blowing through the vents, us breathing, the wind howling outside the car...that is until my phone pinged.

He immediately pulled his hand away. "I gotta go."

Before I could even say goodbye he was out of my car and running to his front door. I sat in my car for a few seconds, just staring outside at the now black sky above the white snow on the ground.

I checked my phone. It was Sonya who had texted me to ask if I'd managed to get the tire changed.

Yeah. I texted back. *How's Erika?*

Good with her family we should talk

k

tonight? tomorrow?

later

I leaned back again and closed my eyes. My life felt as if it was speeding down some long road, and there was no brake to press to calm it, slow it down.

I made it home safely, albeit at a crawl, but I pulled in the driveway and opened the garage to see it empty.

"You're so late," said my mother when I walked into the kitchen. "I was worried."

"I got a flat," I said to my family who, minus Rob, were all sitting down at the dinner table, and now staring at me. Well, not the twins because they were pretty obsessed with their food.

"Oh dear. Why didn't you call?" my mother asked.

"Um, I changed it."

"Atta boy," said my dad. "Did you drop the tire off at the garage on your way home?"

"No." What did he expect of me? I'd barely made it home in the snow. The guy was always one step ahead in his demands.

"You should have dropped it off," he said.

"I'll do it tomorrow."

"You can't drive that car in this weather with a spare. I bet it's got glass in it. Kids are always breaking bottles in that school parking lot."

"Sit down, Gianni," said my mother. "Have some dinner."

I sat down but avoided looking at my father. Sometimes,

he was relentless and picked away at things long after the conversation should have been over.

"How's the play? How's my Danny Zuko?" my mother asked with a let's-change-the-subject cheeriness in her voice.

"About that…" I started. I still hadn't told them I *hadn't* snagged the lead role. I guess I had just conveniently forgotten. It was now or never. "I didn't actually…"

"He's too old to be playing Lego." Nonna waved her fork and whatever she had piled on it splattered on Jerrod who howled and picked it up and threw it at Jason. Typical table trash. My moment to confess was over.

"Oh goodness," said my mother. "I wish she'd turn up those aids." She looked at Nonna. "Nonna," she said patiently. "I said *Zuko* not *Lego*. He's in a musical and we're all going to watch. He's Danny *Zuko*."

Nonna looked at me, her eyes penetrating mine. "You know you have to kiss Olivia Newton-John?"

My father guffawed. "There's nothing wrong with that noggin' of yours, Ma."

The way Nonna looked at me gave me goosebumps, as if she could see right through me. Honestly, she was sort of freaking me out.

"Pass the salad," I said.

The roads had been sanded and cleared by morning and the sun shone in a clear blue sky. The fresh, clean air made the morning bright and gave it some cheer, which I needed. On my way to school I dropped my tire off at the garage. I had to wait for a call from them and then we would figure a time when they could put it back on.

My phone buzzed just as I was parking in my regular spot in the school parking lot. Those guys had left me alone for weeks now. What was the worry now? I looked at my phone. It was the garage calling already.

"Can't fix this one," said the mechanic.

"Why not?" I kept my car running.

"Tire was slashed. You'll need a new one."

"Slashed?"

"Yes. What do you want us to do?"

I ran my hand through my hair. "I need a tire."

"So, new one?"

"Guess so. I have time to come back just before lunch."

"Sounds good, kid. Come on back. We'll fit you in."

I threw my phone on the passenger seat, started my car, and drove out of the parking lot. My father would probably make me pay for this stupid tire or he would moan and tell me he was taking my car away. I drove up and down the side streets, trying to find a spot to park where my car would be totally out of sight.

Because I parked so far away, I had to sprint to the school, but the bell rang before I even made it to the front entrance. I skipped my locker since I already had my books and rushed to my first class, slinking in the back door and nabbing the first seat I could find, which was right beside Sonya.

"Whoa, what's up?" she whispered.

Thankfully, the teacher had his back to the class and was writing something on the board.

"Nothing." I replied.

"Why didn't you call me?"

The teacher turned and started droning on about equations and fortunately, for me anyway, it was easy stuff, because my mind kept wandering to my slashed tire. And then to who'd done the slashing.

After class, Sonya grabbed my arm. "So, what's up?"

I told her how my tire had been slashed as we walked out the door.

"Slashed? In the parking lot?"

She knit her eyebrows together and shook her head. "Who would do something like that?"

"Bunch of kids?" It just came out of my mouth.

"I'm worried about that gang of idiots. They seem to have it in for anyone they think is different."

"Do you think I'm different?" I asked.

"I don't know. Are you?"

"I'm Italian," I said. "My parents are first generation."

She nodded and I wasn't sure that was the answer she wanted. "I guess they've been bugging Bilal too," she said.

"What?" That came out higher than I wanted it to.

"He's Muslim. A huge target for them."

I blew out a big breath or air. "You're right." Here I was, only thinking of me, me, me.

"You never called me last night," she said again.

"Sorry. I had so much homework."

She frowned. "That's never stopped you before."

"It's complicated."

"You can talk to me," she said with a tenderness that made me cringe.

Could I talk to her? Tell her? She deserved to know

something, but right now I just wasn't ready. Anyway, it wasn't anything she wanted to hear, I was sure of that.

"Gianni, what's going on with you?"

I shuffled my books from one arm to the next and looked at the dirty grey tile that made up the school floor. I swear I had a basketball lodged in my throat.

"Talk to me," she urged.

I shook my head. "I've gotta get to my next class."

I glanced at her quickly and the look on her face made my heart shrink. "I'm sorry," I said. "It has nothing to do with you. Everything is…all me."

I turned and escaped down the hall.

"Are you sure it's okay that I hone in on your Best Buddy fun?" Bilal asked on Friday night at the bowling alley. Both of us were trying on ugly bowling shoes. Erika was due to arrive any second.

All week, I hadn't seen much of Bilal because we had different rehearsal schedules. I hadn't spoken to Sonya either, or should I say, she hadn't spoken to me. She went out of her way to avoid me and I didn't blame her. Miss Clark had been rehearsing the T-birds and Pink Ladies a lot and I'd been rehearsing with Erika, keeping her up to speed.

I stood up with my red-and-black shoes on and pretended to do a little tap dance. "What do you think?"

Bilal burst out laughing. "Hilarious!"

"Here they are!" The sound of Karina's voice made me turn. Erika pointed at my shoes.

"Those are funny." She put her hand to her face and laughed. She always thought bowling shoes were funny.

"Don't laugh," I said. "You're going to be wearing them too."

Karina pointed to the bowling shoes behind the counter. "Yeah, but Erika gets pink ones."

"I love pink," said Erika, joyfully clapping her hands. Her excitement was contagious and the darkness inside of me shrivelled away.

"Then let's get you pink!" I said. "What size are you?" I turned to Karina. "Do you want to join us?" I asked.

"No, that's okay. Thanks for asking though." She pulled her gloves out of her pocket and yanked her collar up. "I'm gonna go home. I don't want to leave Mom alone."

"How's your dad?" I asked.

"The tube is helping," said Karina, nodding her head thoughtfully.

"That's good."

"He's going to see me in *Grease*," said Erika.

Karina patted Erika's shoulder. "Let's hope you can make things come true just by wishing." She sat Erika down on the chair and helped her lace up her bowling shoes.

I handed her winter boots to the man behind the counter. "Come on, Erika," I said. "Let's go bowling." I put my arm around her and guided her to the lane we had been given.

When we got there, Bilal made sure the lights were on and our names were on the list. He put Erika's name first.

"You're up, Erika," I said.

We'd been bowling before so she knew exactly what to do. We always played five-pin because the balls were small and easy for her to handle, even if she threw mostly gutter balls. In her pink shoes, she traipsed over to the balls and picked one up.

"*They're going down,*" she said.

Bilal's deep laugh floated through the air. He seemed genuinely happy to be here with me and Erika. She tossed the ball down the lane, and it bounced once then twice before it took its time moving toward the pins. It wasn't going to be a gutter ball this time. It hit the middle pin, teetered, then fell, but no other pins fell with it. Erika didn't care. She jumped up and down, and clapped her hands.

"Yeah, Erika." Bilal pumped his arm in the air.

I was up next and bowled a spare and Bilal followed and nailed a strike. We took our turns and Erika didn't knock down another ball until the fifth frame. By this time, I'd moved to sit beside Bilal by the score table, the move subtle and innocuous, but pleasing to me because our legs were pressed together.

"I got another one," she said, cheering with her hands in the air.

"You're on fire," I said to Erika.

"Actually," Bilal whispered in my ear, "I think I'm the one on fire."

Whoa. I leaned into him so I could feel more of him against me. This small move was done without thinking and at exactly the same time as Erika turned to look at us. She tilted her head and stared at us.

For the rest of the game, Bilal and I stayed away from each other although it was hard. We got to the end of the game and Erika said, "I have to go to the restroom before we go home."

"I can walk you there." Together we walked to the restroom and I told her I would wait outside the door for her.

"I can do this myself," she said.

I nodded. Sometimes I knew I was overprotective with her but better safe than sorry. I would seriously hurt anyone who laid a hand on her.

I decided to wait at the corner, but still with an eye on the restroom door, to give her some independence.

I moved around the corner and leaned up against the wall and, as I stared into space, I wondered what was happening, because *it* was happening, *something* beyond my control. What a night. I was happy, really happy; happier than I'd been in a long time. I know it sounds crazy and melodramatic but it's true. It felt...right.

I heard Bilal before I saw him and he came over to me, holding our jackets. "You're hiding," he said.

"Erika wants her independence." I smiled at him.

I scanned our surroundings.

No one was near us and we were alone in a hallway. When I was convinced there wasn't a soul who could see us, I slowly reached my hand up and touched his face. He tilted his head so his cheek rested in my hand and we stood like that for seconds. Such a simple gesture, a small touch, but the feelings it created were astronomical.

And it felt perfect. So perfect I wanted to sing for joy right there in the hallway.

"No one can know anything about this," whispered Bilal. "And I mean that. It has to stay between us because... it just has to."

"I get it."

"I'm not sure you do. My parents would disown me. What am I saying?" He exhaled. "I would be kicked out of my house."

"You have my word."

"We'd better go."

"Okay," I replied, my voice barely a crack. I touched his face one last time. "I've got to check on Erika."

Then I heard her voice. "I'm done," she said.

CHAPTER THIRTEEN
ERIKA

Gianni was touching Bilal's face. They looked like Karina and Cameron when Cameron was leaving our house and they were standing at the front door and I wasn't supposed to be watching them. I'd seen them even though I was supposed to *butt out*. Yup, Karina liked to tell me that. *Butt out.* Gianni touched Bilal's face like Karina touched Cameron's. And they were both boys. I knew when boys liked each other they were gay because I'd seen it on television, on *Downton Abby*. Karina looooved that show. Karina said there was nothing wrong with boys kissing and that it was just the way it was for some of them. And sometimes girls kissed girls. Yup, she'd told me that when we'd watched it together. Sometimes she explained things about that show cuz I didn't get it but I liked it best when they had big parties and Christmas trees.

"OhheyErika," said Gianni. He was talking really fast. "Bilal has your coat."

Bilal gave me my coat and helped me put it on. Then I put on my favourite plaid tam.

"Time to go," said Gianni. "I told your mom you would be home by nine."

We said goodbye to Bilal, then just Gianni and I walked out to the car. There was a lot of snow and my boots made crunchy noises and footprints.

"Let's make snow angels," I said.

"Great idea," said Gianni. By the sound of his voice I knew he was happy. I couldn't see his face cuz it was too dark.

We had to walk around to find a spot where there was fresh snow but I didn't care. No Siree. I liked walking outside in the snow because everything looked so white and fresh and the air smelled clean, like when I washed my face with soap. I was the one who found a good spot, one where no one had trampled on the snow. We both lay down and moved our arms up and down and up and down. As I moved my arms I stared into the sky and saw so many stars shining, and winking at me, and the moon beaming like it was happy.

"The moon is smiling," I said. "I love making snow angels."

"I haven't made one since I was little," said Gianni.

I moved my arms and legs one more time before I sat up. I wanted to see my angel plus my behind was wet. Yucky. *Gross.*

I stood up and carefully stepped out of my angel so I wouldn't wreck it. When I looked down at it, I saw that it was perfect.

Then I stared at Gianni and he was still making his angel. "You're a slowpoke," I said.

He kept moving his arms like a windshield wiper. Finally, he stopped moving but he didn't get up and instead just stared at the stars as if he was dreaming about something. He wore a big smile on his face and I could see it because of the streetlight. Holy Moly he was smiling!

"Your angel is done," I said.

"We have to make a wish," he said.

I plopped back down into my snow angel's body and looked up at the stars like Gianni was doing. I wished that my daddy wouldn't be sick and could see me in *Grease*.

"Don't tell your wish," he said.

I kept my wish inside my head.

"I love staring at the stars," he said. "They exhilarate me."

I didn't know what *ex-hil-ar*...meant. I stared up at the sky again. "The stars are blinking like they have long eyelashes."

"Erika, sometimes you have the best descriptions." Gianni moved his arms up and down again. Up and down. Up and down.

"I want to make the most perfect angel," he almost sang.

When he stood up it was like he popped up like a jack-in-the-box. I had one of those and I used to wind it up and laugh when it popped. Gianni brushed the snow off his pants. "You make me do the craziest things."

"I didn't make you," I said, getting up too. "You did it yourself."

"Come on, I have to get you home."

When the car was moving I asked him, "How come you don't like Sonya?"

"I do," he said, looking in his mirror at the cars behind him.

I shook my head. "No Way José. Not like Cameron likes Karina."

"No. Not like that," he glanced at me out of the corner of his eye. "Sonya and I are friends."

"You don't talk anymore."

"It's complicated."

My mother used that word with me a lot and usually when she said it I was not supposed to ask any more questions.

I looked out the window and thought about seeing him with Bilal and how they were standing close together and I thought they looked like Karina and Cameron.

"Do you like Bilal instead of Sonya?"

"Um." Gianni breathed, in and out, and the noise sounded loud in the car.

"I think Richard is *hot*," I said.

Gianni laughed. "Where'd you get that one from?"

"Some girls in the hall said it," I said.

"I think you're doing well with the dances for *Grease*," he said. "Next week we should work on the third song."

"I like the last song. Sonya dresses in her black outfit," I said. "She's going to look so pretty and *hot*."

"*Hot*. You like that word."

"A boy in my gym class thinks Claire is *hot*. I heard him say it."

"Well, I will agree with you: Sonya will look hot. *You* have a costume fitting next week too. It's on the schedule. You get your poodle skirt and a prom dress too, I think."

"On Monday." I clapped. "I hope my poodle skirt is yellow."

"No matter what colour it is, you're going to look great," he said.

"You should like Sonya cuz she likes you and she's my best friend."

My house was so quiet when I walked in the door. Gianni walked me right to the door but didn't come in. We just said goodbye on the step. When I went inside, I didn't like how no one greeted me at the back door and asked me about bowling. No Siree. Karina had texted Gianni and told him she was home.

"Hello!" I yelled. Where was she? I didn't like being alone.

"Erika." I heard Karina coming down the hall.

"Where were you?"

"Daddy's sick."

"Why?" My lip started to quiver.

"He has a cold and he's having a hard time breathing. Mom wants to take him to the hospital."

"No!" I shook my head back and forth. "I didn't like it there. It smelled."

"Erika, if he has to go, he has to go." Karina squeezed her hands together and her face looked scared, like before she wrote big exams, but even worse.

I rushed over to her and hugged her. She wrapped her arms around me and I pressed my head against her. She put her chin on the top of my head and I could feel it trembling. I let go of her and reached for her hand.

She squeezed my fingers then she lifted my chin and looked me in the eyes. "What would I do without you?"

We walked down the hall to the door of my mom and dad's bedroom, which was closed.

"We should knock," whispered Karina.

I put my knuckles up to the door and rapped lightly. *Knock. Knock. Knock.* Then I pressed my ear to the door. When I heard my mother's footsteps, I stepped back and waited for her to open the door.

"Can we come in?" Karina asked.

"Sure," said Mom.

Karina and I held hands again as we walked in and I liked that she wanted to hold my hand. All my life she'd held my hand, like when we walked across the street or went into crowded shopping malls, and even at Disneyland. We walked and walked at Disneyland and she held my hand. She never let it go.

Together we walked to Daddy's bedside. I could hear him breathing, in and out, and the sound was like paper being crinkled. It hurt my ears. As I got closer to him I could see his chest rising up and down and up and down. It wasn't moving fast or slow but like the steady beat of a drum. I'd done drums at school in music. His eyes were closed and his face looked like someone had coloured it grey.

I stood beside him and took his hand and it felt cold. I didn't squeeze it but just held onto it. Karina put her hand on his arm.

"Daddy, we're here for you." Karina sniffled. Then she turned to my mother. "What can we do to help him breathe better?"

My mother sighed and it sounded loud. "I called the doctor," she said. "He said to monitor him and if his breathing gets any more laboured I'm to call an ambulance. I'm supposed to keep the vaporizer on to help him breathe. If it's just a cold he'll be okay. We just have to make sure it doesn't turn into pneumonia. I'm hoping he'll be better by morning."

I didn't understand what *la-boured* meant or *vap-or*…or *pneu-mon-i-a* meant. But I did know what *better* meant.

"He won't get *better*." I stated. I looked up at my mother. "You told me that. Did you lie to me?" Why would she say he would get better? No one is supposed to lie.

"Erika," my mother gently put her arm around me. "Daddy will always have ALS and he won't get better from that, but if he gets over this cold he could breathe better. That's what I meant by better."

Suddenly, my father started making funny noises in his throat and I didn't like how it sounded, like water was bubbling.

"Mom, that doesn't sound good," said Karina, her voice higher than normal.

My mother rushed to my father's side and rolled his head so that his ear was on the pillow. Dribble came out of his mouth, landing on his pillow, making it wet.

"This is actually okay," said my mother. "A good sign. We're getting some fluid out, which could be blocking his breathing."

He needed a blanket. "Excuse me," I said.

"Where are you going?" Karina asked.

I didn't tell her but just went to the family room and got the fuzzy brown blanket. I came back to my parents' bedroom and put the blanket over his other blankets. "I made a snow angel tonight and made a wish," I said.

Karina put her arm around me.

"I wished he could see me in *Grease*," I said. I didn't want to keep my wish a *secret*.

"I hope your wish comes true," said Karina.

"You make a wish too," I said.

"I want him to see me graduate. That's my wish," said Karina.

When I woke up in the morning I wanted to see my Dad before breakfast. I liked that his breathing wasn't so loud. I stroked his forehead.

"Morning, Erika." I could barely hear him speak.

"It's Saturday," I said. "When you get out of bed, do you want to watch television? We could watch *Grease*."

"Yes." His word was quiet but I heard him.

"I'm going to get my Honey Nut Cheerios," I said, "and I won't put milk on them. And I'm going to stay in my jammies. I'll get you a blanket to keep you warm. That's my job."

My father and I watched *Grease* until it was time for me to go to hip hop class. In my bedroom, I put on my new bandana that my mother had bought me at Wal-Mart and I made sure I wore it on my forehead just like *Corey did*.

My teacher Corey noticed my new headband.

"Cool headband, Erika."

"Thanks. My dad is sick."

"I'm sorry to hear that." He jerked his head towards the dance room. "Let's dance. Dancing can take your mind off things. It's like therapy."

Ther-a-py? I took speech therapy but dancing wasn't talking.

But dancing did make me forget about my dad being sick. Corey taught us a new move where we had to go in a circle, round and round, moving out feet in and out and in and out until we ended up at the front of the room again. I called it a spin. Jimmy called it a tornado and went around twice, sometimes three times.

When I got home I right away went into the family room where my dad was sitting in his chair. "Daddy, watch—"

I stopped. Something was different. I stared at his wheelchair. His head wasn't drooping cuz he had something new on his wheelchair.

"What's *that?*" I asked.

"A neck brace."

I just stared at it. "I like it," I said. "I can see your eyes."

"Dance for me," he said.

I showed him my new spin move. When my mother came into the family room, she said, "You're doing great at this hip hop dance."

"Yup. Watch this." I did the spin move again.

"Bravo," said my dad.

"It's my turn to make dinner tonight," I said. "I have two jobs tonight." I held up two fingers.

"I'm proud of you," he said.

"And I'm proud of *you*," I replied.

On Monday, I walked from my locker to rehearsal with Gianni. I knew it was costume day so I tried to walk faster. I couldn't wait to see my poodle skirt and prom dress. Yippee! When we entered the drama room there was a big, long rack of colourful costumes and they were all on hangers. I wondered which one was mine. My tummy felt bubbly and I wanted my costume now. Miss Clark clapped her hands and called us all in to the middle.

"I would like to do this in an organized fashion. Rianne is going to be our costume girl."

Rianne stepped forward and gave everyone a wave. We all waved back. I had gone to middle school with Rianne and she had been my science partner in grade four.

"She's *classic*," I said to Gianni.

"That's a new one," he whispered. "Let's listen to Miss Clark."

"I will call your name," said Miss Clark, "and Rianne will hand you your costume or costumes for some of you in dual roles. When you get your lot, please go to the change room, and try them on. Then come out and show us what they look like. If you have a costume that doesn't fit, which shouldn't happen because everyone was measured, still come out because I need to see if we can do alterations. No eating or drinking while in costume." She held up her hands. "I will repeat, no eating or drinking while in costume."

My whole body tingled like I was a buzzing alarm clock. I could hardly wait for my name to be called. When Miss Clark called mine I ran right over to her.

"Go, Erika," said Richard.

I clapped I was so excited. Yippee! She handed me a pretty yellow skirt with red on it too. Inside I felt as if I was bubbling like ginger ale after the can had just been opened. There was a sweater to match and it was red and my hair ribbon was shiny and red just like my sweater. Then Rianne handed me a frilly red dress too.

"This is your costume for the prom song," she said.

"It's pretty!" I squealed.

I turned to Gianni. "I got two costumes!"

He gave me a thumbs up.

I held on to my costumes tightly. I didn't want to drop them.

Miss Clark looked over my head and said, "Sonya, since we've organized your costumes already, I would like you to help Erika."

Sonya walked me to the change room and when we got there she helped me undress.

She handed me my skirt first. "I love the colour," she said.

I put on the skirt, then I put on the sweater, but I needed help with the buttons cuz they were so small.

"You look awesome!" Sonya clapped little claps. "Twirl," she said.

I twirled and my skirt looked like the biggest, most colourful fan I'd ever seen in my whole life. I laughed and twirled until I got dizzy.

Sonya grabbed me by the shoulders and stopped me. "You're going to keel over," she said, laughing too.

"Do I look pretty?"

"So pretty! Come on." She took my hand and walked me over to the mirror. "Look at you. Everything fits perfectly."

I put my hands on my cheeks.

Sonya took some of my hair, pulled it back, and tied the ribbon around it. "I heard they have a hairdresser who said she would help with hair."

"Let's go show Miss Clark," said Sonya. "Then we'll come back and put on your prom dress."

"And Gianni too," I said.

"Yes, and Gianni." She tried to sound cheerful but I don't think she was.

"Are you sad because he likes Bilal instead of you?"

She squished her eyebrows together. "Why would you say that?"

Suddenly, I felt really funny and not happy anymore. "I dunno," I said. I stared at the floor.

"Erika, why did you say that?" Sonya asked me again. Her voice was kinda quiet.

I didn't answer.

"Erika?"

"They were touching," I said.

She lifted my chin and stared me in the eyes. "It's okay to tell me that. But don't say that to anyone else, okay?"

"Is it a secret?

"Kind of. And it's Gianni's secret." She looked away from me but I could see by her still squished eyebrows that she was thinking hard about something. But then she looked back at me, and said, "Come on, we need to show everyone how awesome you look."

"Okee-dokee." We walked back to the drama room and when I walked in, Gianni was there in his funny Eugene costume, with his pants pulled up really high with black things that I think were called *sus-pen-ders,* and he wore black glasses that were taped at the nose.

"You look fantastic!" he said to me.

"You look funny," I said to him. Then I twirled like I did in the change room, my skirt flaring out like a huge umbrella this time. I didn't twirl as long because I didn't want to get dizzy.

When I was done, Gianni made a Eugene face and I laughed and so did Sonya, and that made me feel good.

Sonya and I went back to the change room.

"I think I should help you with this red dress," she said. "It's a tricky dress and needs to go over your head."

I took off my poodle skirt and hung it on the hanger and my sweater too.

"Hold up your arms," said Sonya.

I did and I felt the dress slip down my body. I put my arms in the arm holes and Sonya did up the zipper in the back. *Zip. Zip.* I looked down and saw the red shiny fabric go all the way to the ground. It made me feel like a real princess and not just the pretend princess like I played when I was with Gianni.

"Erika, you look so incredible! That dress is perfect on you."

"Like a princess."

"You are *soooo* right," said Sonya. "That's exactly what you look like."

Again, she guided me to the big mirror. I stared at myself then I clasped my hands in front of my chest. "It's the prettiest dress ever." And it was. It was red and shiny and had puffy sleeves that had bows. It was wide at the bottom and looked like a big, red, pretty bell.

This time when I walked out Richard whistled. "Er-i-ka. You look like royalty."

I grabbed the sides and made it swish. I liked Richard cuz he said nice things to me.

After everyone had their costumes fitted we had to get undressed and put them back on their special hangers. Rianne put all the costumes back on the rack. Miss Clark glanced at the clock.

"We have enough time to run through our third dance again. It's still not quite cutting it for me."

Gianni had practised with me and I knew it off by heart. We went over and over and over the dance and after thirty minutes I was sweating so much it was dripping down my face and my legs were tired. Miss Clark was still shaking her head at us.

"Let's do it again!" she yelled, and I put my hands to my ears.

The music began and we all started dancing. We were part way through when Miss Clark turned the music off and clapped her hands.

"Stop." She rubbed her forehead, like she had a huge itch. "This isn't working. Something is off." She paced back and forth and back and forth. The heels on her shoes went *click, clack, click, clack.*

"Okay," she said rubbing her forehead, "at this point I'm open to suggestions."

I thought about the dance and I thought about my hip hop class. I put up my hand. "I have a *sug-ges-tion,*" I said. I kinda spit when I said that big word.

Beside me, Gianni whispered through his teeth, "Not the moonwalk, Erika. Not now."

I turned to Gianni and said, "Well, duh. Not the moonwalk silly." I turned back to Miss Clark. "I know a spin move from my hip hop class."

"Hip hop?" Miss Clark made a funny face.

"I'll show you." I remembered every step that Corey had taught me and showed everyone what I had learned. When I finished I knew I had done the best I ever had. "It's good with music," I said.

The cast members clapped and whistled and cheered.

"You know," said Miss Clark, like she was thinking deep inside her head. She shook her finger as she thought. "That isn't such a bad idea." I knew enough not to talk and interrupt her brain from working properly.

Finally, she said, "We *could* add a bit of hip hop at the end. It would be different and give it a punch."

Suddenly, her face looked like someone had turned on a light that was really bright. "Erika, that is just a super-duper fantastic idea!" She almost squealed in excitement. "That's what it needs! Spunk."

Miss Clark's eyes were bright and shiny now and I knew she was happy with my *sug-ges-tion.*

"*Super-duper fan-tas-tic,*" I said. Then I gave her the hip hop peace sign just like we did in class.

The room filled with this crazy laughter. Gianni patted my shoulder and I grinned up at him. Then I did my moonwalk, tipping my hat in the end, making everyone really, really laugh, including me.

CHAPTER FOURTEEN
GIANNI

I almost groaned out loud when Erika spoke up and said she had an idea. Miss Clark was seriously ready to erupt and spew hot lava over every one of us. We'd gone over and over the dance and it was still a nightmare.

And I knew Erika. If her suggestion was going to make Miss Clark lose her cool even a little, which was totally possible, (not because she was mean but because we were close to opening night), Erika would be crushed and would possibly cry or worse.

I held my breath. But then Erika, as only she can do, surprised all of us by suggesting some hip hop moves. And Miss Clark loved the idea! She got the gleam in her eye that creative types get when they recognize a great idea has been hatched. The corner of my mouth lifted at Erika's unpredictability, and my stupidity.

And just like that, we were all practising a hip hop spin move to put in the dance and, you know what? It was magical. Amanda and Claire took the reins and were able to come up with something on the spot, with Erika's help, of course. It gave the entire dance energy—made it "funky," as Erika would say— but in this cool kind of offbeat '50s way. Plus, it had the element of surprise.

"This is going to be so cool," Amanda said to Erika after rehearsal, holding her hand up in the air. Erika responded with the biggest high five I'd ever seen her give. She darn near knocked Amanda over.

Sonya came up to stand beside me. "What a girl."

"I thought for sure she was going to do the moonwalk," I said, "and I was sweating buckets hoping Miss Clark wouldn't unleash."

"I did too," admitted Sonya. "I was holding my breath. I knew Miss Clark was *stressed*."

"Stressed is probably too mild of a word," I said.

"Speaking of stressed," she said quietly, "You want to talk sometime? I miss you."

"I miss you too," I said, lowering my voice. And I did. I missed talking to her about the most trivial things and the deep things too. But I didn't want to lead her on again because that wasn't fair. I glanced at Bilal, but he seemed to be making a point of looking anywhere but in my direction.

"Who wants to go celebrate Erika and her amazing hip hop moves?" Richard yelled to the group through cupped hands, his voice booming through the room.

Everyone cheered and the noise was deafening. Erika put her hands to her ears.

Sonya poked me in the arm. "I'll save you a seat," she whispered.

Like a swirl of wind, Erika ran over to me and tugged on my jacket. "Gimme your phone. Gimme your phone. Please. I have to tell Karina I'm going to Starbucks."

I pulled out my phone and once I found Karina's contact info, I handed it over. With full concentration she stared at the phone, tapped out a text message, and hit send before handing it back to me.

After we'd gathered coats and hats and books, Erika and I walked out to my car. I could see Bilal walking ahead of us. He'd avoided me all week and when I'd texted him to ask what was wrong, he'd said, "Leave me alone. I can't be seen with you."

"Bilal," I called out.

He turned.

"Do you need a ride?"

"It's okay. I'm heading home."

"You're not gonna come *cel-e-brate* my hip hop?" Erika asked.

That stopped Bilal in his tracks, literally since there was snow, and he waited for us to catch up to him. The closer we got to him the more my heart raced. Once we stood beside him, it felt like there was this invisible concrete wall that separated us.

Bilal focused his attention on Erika and wagged his finger at her. "You drive a hard bargain."

"Please," she said. "You're Kenickie. The *super cool* T-bird." Of course, because she was on a roll, she added some hip hop hand gestures.

"Okay, okay, but just for you."

When we got to my car, Bilal opened the back door and slid in and Erika hopped in the front to ride shotgun. The entire way there we talked about the show and nothing else, and that was a good thing because at least we had something to talk about. Inside the coffee shop, I got in line to get drinks. Sonya waved to me, showing me that she had saved a seat for me and Erika. Bilal sat down at the other end of the table, as far away from me as possible.

I won't deny it, Bilal sitting on the other side of the room hurt like stink. I get how he wanted to hide us, or what I thought was us, which in a way wasn't really us, but at least he could allow us to sneak a glance or a touch. Was I asking too much?

I got our drinks and sat down beside Sonya. She squeezed my forearm.

"Erika's crushing on Richard," she whispered.

"I know."

"I told her that a relationship was always better when the couple starts as friends first."

"That's good advice."

"I also told her that sometimes friends can't be a couple but they can still be friends."

I sipped my coffee.

In a low voice Sonya she said, "She told me something that I want to talk to you about later."

"Okay."

"I think maybe I understand something about you now."

My heart thudded. My throat dried. Then, I don't know why I did what I did, but I stood up, almost knocking the table over, and bellowed, "Let's hear it for Erika." I raised my coffee. "Here's to her brilliant dance moves!"

The days flew by as we were doubling up on rehearsals. The show was less than two weeks away and both Miss Clark and Mr. Warner were freaking out and worried about timing and props and costumes and actors who were calling for lines and forgetting lyrics and not entering and exiting on time. Like Richard. Even Sonya was getting frustrated with him.

After one rehearsal, to my surprise, Richard approached me. "Hey, can you help me?"

I shrugged. "Sure. What do you need help with?"

"I'm struggling with the one song. Danny's love song. I can't get the notes." He sounded extremely tense and he kept running his hands through his hair.

"Okay," I said. I scanned the room and saw that it had emptied. "We could stay now, if you have time."

"Oh boy, I've got time." He nodded as he exhaled. "That'd be great."

We waited for the room to clear before we put on the music. Of course, I had every song of his memorized. He sang for me and I listened to his tone and when I heard his pitch veer, I stopped. "I want you to think of the note as a whole and sing in the middle of it."

We went over and over his pitch problems and, bingo, he suddenly got it. When he did, he jumped for joy and gave me a bear hug that darn near crushed me. Afraid to feel something, (because, well, he was *hot*), I pushed him away and pretended to be bashful and that's when I saw Bilal lurking by the door. A moment later, he disappeared.

"Hey, I gotta go," I said to Richard. "But let me know if you need help again."

"Thanks a million, dude. I owe you one."

I quickly gathered up my things and hurried out of the room. Once I was in the halls, I scanned them, looking for Bilal. Nowhere. Crap. I knew where his locker was so I sprinted down the empty hallways. Still nowhere.

The bus! I zipped out the front doors of the school and immediately saw him standing at the bus shelter, alone. I took off at a fast clip, my sneakers barely giving me the traction I needed in the snow, but I didn't care and I slipped and I slid until…I stood in front of him.

"Bilal," I said, panting.

Bilal scanned our surroundings. "Not here." He hissed the words through his teeth.

He abruptly pivoted and headed toward the back of the school. I followed. We walked down a worn path for a bit and ventured behind the school to a secluded little alcove.

"You're avoiding me," I said.

"You don't get it," he snapped. "I have to."

I wanted desperately to ask, 'Why?" but I knew why and I guess I understood. "Ok," I said. What else could I say?

When he didn't respond or look at me, I said, "We have to make an effort to at least talk now and again, for the sake of the show. Tension ruins productions."

He kicked at the snow. And kicked and kicked. Finally he said, "I hated seeing you with Richard tonight."

"I'm just helping him."

He shook his head and kicked a huge chunk of ice that pinged against the snow fence. "It's just that my feelings make me know…what I don't want to know. It can't be like this for me. It just can't." Another kick, and another big chunk of ice flew through the air. This time the ping echoed.

I tried to swallow to clear my throat so I could say something. He sounded so desperate and I wanted to reassure him that everything would be fine—but how could I when I didn't know if that was the truth?

Silence swirled around us. Finally I said, "I understand."

We locked eyes. I longed to move closer, feel his breath on my face, his hands on my skin.

"My bus will be here soon," he said, backing away from me.

"I can drive you."

"No."

As soon as we came out of our secluded area a car screamed by us, and a container thudded to the ground at our feet, splashing a crappy blue ice drink all over the sidewalk. The smell of alcohol wafted through the air.

"Terrorist!" A voice yelled from the car.

"Get out of our country!" another voice called out. "Go home!"

I looked at the stain the blue sugar created and how it spread like a blob through the snow. And then I got it. He had to worry about being targeted for being Muslim *and* gay.

"Idiots," said Bilal with venom in his voice. The dark look on his face would scare the crap out of me in a dark alley. I'd never heard him sound so bitter.

"If they find out about *this,*" he pointed to me and him in jerky movements, "I'm done."

"Have…those guys…been harassing you for long?"

"Every day," he said. "Every damn day."

I thought about my slit tires. "What have they been doing to you?"

"Ah, just a little shit in my locker. Piss in my shoes. Spit on my gym clothes. Oh, and threats about how they're going to catch me and beat the crap out of me, make my pretty face a mess."

"Wow. I didn't know it was that bad for you."

I'd only had one incident and then everything stopped. Except my tire being slashed and there was absolutely no proof it was them.

"Oh yeah," he muttered. "It's bad. I've thought about switching schools. But that would let them win. Plus they'd still find me. Their targets aren't just at our school." I heard the bus squealing down the street, coming toward us.

"Look. I'm not gay. I'm just…confused." The bus doors opened and closed, and he was gone.

I stood there, letting snowflakes land on my skin. Softly, gently, falling. When I looked down I saw the fluffy white flakes landing on the splattered, blue ice drink, where they turned from white to blue.

December 1st arrived, and it also happened to be the first Thursday of the month, meaning we had a Best Buddies meeting. The Hooping It Up event was on the following Monday, only four days away. And opening night was nine days after that, and then the show would run for three nights.

Erika and I walked into the Best Buddies meeting together and sat in the seats we always sat in. Everyone in the Best Buddies program sat in the same seats every meeting. Except today, I noticed a new blonde girl sitting in a seat at the front.

"Welcome to our last meeting before Christmas everyone," said Justin. "Before we begin, I'd like to introduce you to Madeline. She's new and is going to be my Best Buddy.

She loves horses. Right Madeline?" Justin smiled at her, an actual happy smile, which was kind of rare because he was such a serious dude.

Madeline nodded.

"Okay, onto today's agenda. The Hooping It Up event is shaping up great, thanks to Willa and Gloria who've been heading the committee. Willa, do you want to tell us what you have planned so far?"

"Well, for one, my band is going to rock out," she said. "We've even been working on some Christmas tunes."

"Play *The Little Drummer Boy*," said Erika. "It's my favourite."

"Right on," said Willa. "That's one we've been working on. Just for you, girl."

"We're also going to set up stations where people can try to shoot the basket in the hoop and if they get so many in a row they get a prize," continued Willa. "We've managed to get some cool prizes. For the finale we have the volleyball teams, notice I said *teams* plural, playing the soccer *teams*. They will combine their male and female *teams*. No sexism here. Who wants to ref?"

I looked over at Erika. "You want to ref with me?"

"Yup! I wanna ref."

Don stood up and pumped his arms. "I wanna ref."

"We'll sign up," said Marcie.

"Perfect," said Justin. Then he turned to me. "Did you bring the tickets for *Grease*?"

"I did." I pulled them out of my coat pocket. Each cast member had ten to sell. For me that wasn't hard because my entire family was coming, including Nonna, even though I still hadn't told them I wasn't Danny Zuko. Since I had left it so late, I thought I might as well wait for opening night. Surprise!

Erika rummaged through her backpack, yanking out her envelope and whipping up her hand like she was a hockey goalie making a save. "I brought mine too!"

Mr. Warner summoned the cast to meet for an extra acting rehearsal, no dancing, just acting. Being Eugene, I wasn't in every scene so I sat back and watched the others do their thing, and noted that Bilal was brilliant as Kenickie and Richard sufficed as Danny. His song was better, thanks to our extra practising, but he kept stumbling over his lines. Nerves. Pre-show jitters.

Although I watched the entire scene, my gaze kept drifting to Bilal. All week he'd avoided me and it was as if it pained him to even say hello.

"Eugene, you ready?" Mr. Warner bellowed.

I jumped up and put on my Eugene face, strolling on set in my Eugene walk, shoulders slouched, feet out to the side and hollowed stomach. I was going to kill this role.

After rehearsal, Sonya gathered up her bag. "Hey, Eugene," she said. "Walk out with me?"

I gave Bilal a sidelong glance, but his back was still turned. When Amanda sidled up beside him he put his hand on the small of her back, an intimate gesture.

"Ok," I said to Sonya.

Outside, the sky was pitch black already, and dramatically noir, as the moon was only a slight sliver in its waxing crescent phase. I loved this time of year, the early dark.

"Erika and I made snow angels one night," I said, staring upwards at the stars.

"Oh, how fun."

"I made a wish."

"Did it come true?"

"No." I sighed and jingled my keys.

Sonya stopped walking and grabbed my arm, making me stop as well. "Look," she said, "You keep avoiding me. Enough."

"I'm sorry."

"Erika said something to me, *weeks ago*, and then everything kind of made sense."

I grimaced. Yes, it was time for me to have this conversation and, yes, she was right that it was long overdue. Sonya *had* been at me for weeks to talk and I had stalled her again and again but here we were, standing in the winter air, and I was suddenly done trying to avoid her any longer.

I nodded. "What did she say?"

"She asked me if I was upset that you liked Bilal better than me."

"Wow." I blew stale air out of my lungs and into the crisp clear night.

"She's smart," said Sonya softly.

"I know how smart she is." I shoved my hands in my pockets and hunched up my shoulders. "Look, I'm just...so confused." My voice cracked.

"Gianni, I'm okay about all of this." She touched my arm. "I've got thick skin when it comes to guys. Honest. What I'm not okay about is you not talking to me about it."

"I'm sorry."

"If that's the truth then I understand and if it makes you feel better, I feel so much better about your rejection. I guess I just liked you because you were nice and I wanted a nice guy after all the jerks I've dated."

I finally made eye contact. "You deserve someone who treats you well."

"Whatever. We're talking about you."

I blew out a rush of air. "Please—don't tell anyone. I'm just not ready for *everyone* to know. And...I don't think he'd... he'd forgive me."

"It's more of a struggle for him?"

"It's different for him. And maybe he doesn't even know yet or maybe he'll never know or maybe he's not." I shrugged. "I'm not him so I can't say. But I do know if the rumour spread, he would hate me."

"So...you know for sure? I mean, about you?"

"It's a lot harder to figure out then you think. It's so mystifying and at times unclear and like one gigantic puzzle. I think I've taken a baby step forward." This time when I sighed it was loud. "But to answer your question, yeah, I guess I do know about me. I told my brother."

"You are who you are, Gianni. And none of this changes the fact that you're the nicest guy in the school." She lifted her eyebrows. "Except when you blow me off. I'm still mad about that." She playfully smacked me across the arm.

"I've been a jerk these past couple of weeks."

"I wish I could be more mad at you."

"But you're not?" I finally gave her a little smile.

"You're going through a lot."

"Thanks," I said.

"You're welcome."

She wrapped one arm around my waist and rested her head against my arm. "You'll handle it, Gianni," she said. "And everyone will accept you because you'll still be you."

We disengaged and I jerked my head to my car. "You're probably cold."

She hugged her body. "Yeah, I should get home and study."

We walked toward her car. Mine was still parked on the street. "Call me if you need help," I said. "With the homework that is."

"Oh man, I've missed your help." She unlocked the doors to her car.

"You can come over if you want," I said.

Her eyes lit up. "Has your mom been baking lately?"

"Ha ha. It's her middle name." I opened her car door for her. "I'm freaked about what my father will say."

She turned to me. "He loves you. He'll accept you."

"Yeah. That's what my brother says but you never know how someone will react. I can't even tell them I'm Eugene in the show. They think I'm Zuko."

"What? You didn't tell them you're Eugene?" She playfully slapped me, again. "You'd better tell them before opening night. Why would you not tell them?"

I shrugged. "I tried once and then I forgot I guess. Too much on my mind."

"Tell them!"

"Nah, let them be surprised," I said.

"No! At least your mother deserves to know." She looked around the parking lot. "Where's your car?"

"I park it on the street."

"Because of your flat. Did you ever find out who slashed it?"

"No."

"Get in. I'll drive you to it."

As we drove out to the street where my car was parked, she said, "Those guys are getting worse, you know. I heard some Iranian girl at another school got her head scarf ripped off. I bet it was them."

"They're on Bilal's case for being Muslim," I said.

Deep in thought, she nodded. "Their targets do seem more racial and religious lately."

"There's my car," I pointed.

She pulled up beside my car. "We've got to stop them."

I sighed. "I know." I paused for a second before getting out. "But it's one of those things that if you tell anyone without any proof then nothing happens, there are zero results. Circle, retreat, circle, retreat," I said. "That's how they operate. And too many people are afraid to come forward. It's scary but they have to almost be caught in the act."

"There has to be a way," she said.

"Let me know when you figure it out," I said.

"Gianni." She put her hand on my arm. "Is he breaking your heart?"

"Something like that," I said before getting out of her car.

CHAPTER FIFTEEN
ERIKA

"What are you watching?" I asked Karina. I was tired like a dog that had run and run in a park. But I was tired from dancing and dancing and not from running. I wanted all the practising to be over. Gianni had practised with me a lot. I wanted to wear my poodle skirt and prom dress and dance in front of people.

"A movie," replied Karina.

My dad was wearing that funny thing on his nose and he wasn't even sleeping. My mom said it was a mask but it wasn't like a real mask, not a Halloween mask. I thought it looked like nose plugs. I wore nose plugs when I went swimming. And it had a tube and the tube gave him oxygen. After his cold he couldn't breathe the same and his ribs had gone up and down and all that breathing sounded like crunching potato chips. He needed extra oxygen like I had to have extra *re-hear-sals*. I know what oxygen is because I learned about it in science.

"I'm pooped."

"Practise is good," said my dad.

When I was little and learning to read words, my dad said I needed to keep trying even when I threw the book on the floor. He went over and over the words with me. We practised. I reached up and touched his mask.

"You're wearing this to watch TV," I said. I touched his mask.

"It helps," he said.

"You already have a blanket."

"Yes," he said.

Since I didn't have to do my job of getting my dad a blanket, I sat down on the side of the sofa that was next to him. "I don't want this movie to be scary," I said.

"It's not," said Karina. "It's a comedy. You'll like it." She plumped up her pillow.

I sat between Karina and my dad.

"I've heard *Grease* is going great," said Karina. "Someone said the costumes are amazing and the set design crew have done a fantastic job. The senior art class did the design."

"It looks like a real *soda* shop," I said.

Karina stretched her legs out in front of her. I liked it when she watched television with me. "Are you excited for the Best Buddy event Monday? It's kicking off our games week."

"I'm gonna sink baskets."

"I bet you will."

She stopped talking and watched the television. A girl kissed a boy on the movie and I stared at them kissing.

"Gianni doesn't like Sonya," I said, looking at the television again.

"Really? Since when?"

"He likes Bilal."

"Excuse me?" Karina sat up straight, like a pole, and picked up the remote. She turned the volume down.

"No! Don't do that. I wanna watch," I said.

"Not until you explain what you just said."

"You're bossy." I crossed my arms and stared at the television.

"Where did you hear this?" said Karina. "Did someone say something to you?"

I still didn't look at her.

Then I remembered that Sonya had told me not to tell. *Oh no. Oh no. Oh no.* Now I really didn't want to talk to Karina about this. I kept staring at the television.

"Did *Gianni* tell you that?"

I shook my head and I knew she was staring at me cuz I could see her out of the side of my eyes. Her eyes were open wide and it was almost as if she was wearing a question mark on her forehead.

"Talk to me," she said more quietly.

I thought and thought. No one told me. And I didn't hear anyone talking. I had seen them touch. "He touched Bilal like you touch Cameron," I said.

"Look at me for a second, okay?"

She didn't sound bossy anymore so I pushed my lips together and looked at her.

"It's important that you don't tell anyone else that. It's okay that you told me but it's not up to you to tell anyone else."

I didn't say anything back.

"Sometimes boys like boys. You know that. But you shouldn't be telling people about Gianni and Bilal if you don't know the truth absolutely for sure. This is something Gianni will tell everyone when *he* wants to. It's his *personal business.*"

I looked down at the sofa. My mom always told me that other people's *personal business* was their business, not mine.

Karina touched my arm. "Erika, it's okay that you told me

because I'm your family. Just don't say anything to anyone else."

"Is it a secret?" I asked. "Sonya said it was."

"Sonya's right. It's not a bad secret. But this one is Gianni's secret and maybe Bilal's too."

"That's what Sonya said too." I shook my head back and forth and back and forth. "I don't like secrets," I said.

"Secrets can be hard to understand. But you understand what I'm saying, don't you, Erika?"

I nodded and then put my cheek on my dad's arm. I didn't want to talk about this anymore.

"Listen to your sister," he said. "She's right."

On Monday I wore my Best Buddies t-shirt to school. It was Hooping It Up day. Yippee! But my classes were so long and I had a hard time listening to what my teachers were saying. On and on they talked. So many people were coming to the Hooping It Up event. Posters were pinned on bulletin boards all over the school and I was even on the poster. All day I was like a celebrity! Every time I saw a poster, I saw me! I stopped so many people to show them my face. Yeah! I looked pretty too. All the Best Buddies were on the poster. My heart was jumping under my t-shirt, like a Mexican Jumping Bean. Holy Moly I was excited.

Green and red balloons were put up all around the gymnasium. I clapped when I saw them. My dad bought me yellow and pink balloons for my birthday when I was seven. And green and red meant Christmas!

Posters and signs that I had helped make were all over the

walls. At the far end of the gymnasium, a door was wide open and I saw Willa come through it, carrying a big drum.

"We get Santa hats." I pulled on Gianni's arm. "Justin has them."

But Gianni didn't budge from his spot because he was staring at a group of boys on the other side of the gymnasium. *Uh oh. Uh oh. Uh oh.* The mean boys were in the gym. My tummy started to turn topsy-turvy. And I felt my insides shaking. They had come in the same door as Willa with her drum. I pulled on Gianni's arm again, only harder this time.

He turned and I didn't like how his eyes looked so big.

"Let's get our Santa hats," he said. "Ho Ho Ho." He tried to smile and sound jolly like Santa does at the mall.

We walked across the gym, away from the boys, and over to Justin who had a box full of red hats with fluffy white parts. Madeline and Sarah helped Justin hand out our hats and I put mine on my head right away, and I let the puff part of it, (I called it the puff), sit over my shoulder. I knew it was supposed to be called a pom-pom but I think it looked like a cotton puff. Yup. A cotton puff.

I watched the clock and it took thirty minutes to finish putting up all the decorations and make the gymnasium look *awe-some!* Willa set up a microphone and all kinds of big black boxes that Gianni told me were amp-li-fliers. *Amp-li-fliers.* That's a big word.

By the time we had finished setting everything up the mean boys had left. They went out the same door they'd come in. I was glad they were gone. Yup. I was. And I hoped they weren't coming back. "I'm glad those mean boys left," I said to Gianni.

Gianni looked at me with his *focus* look. "If you see them," he said, "promise me you'll walk the other way. As fast as you can."

I nodded.

Gianni touched my shoulder and smiled at me. "Come on, let's have some fun."

The gymnasium filled up with so many kids, and teachers too, and the noise got louder and louder with basketballs bouncing and Willa's band playing and kids cheering when they put the ball in the basket. My tummy bubbled and felt good. Willa's band played *The Little Drummer Boy* and *Jingle Bells*. I sang along cuz I knew all the words to both those songs.

"Erika, let's play basketball," said Gianni. He seemed a lot happier than before and I didn't see the mean boys anymore. I hoped they'd gone home for dinner.

He winked at me. "I know you can win a prize."

Yup. I could win a prize. We walked over to the basketball place where Karina was working. She was throwing the basketball to the person who was playing and she was giving out the prizes when someone put the basketball in the hoop.

"Erika wants to play," said Gianni.

"Okay." Karina threw a ball to me. I missed catching it but Gianni was as fast as a cheetah and he ran behind me and scooped it up.

"Stand here, Erika," he said. "And hold the ball like this."

"Okee-dokee."

He put it in my hands and moved my hands around the ball. Then he arched it up in front of my face. "Now bend your legs a little and throw it."

With his help we pushed the ball forward and into the air. It flew and hit the rim and bounced but it didn't go in.

"You've got two more chances," he said. "Let's do it again."

The next one went in! *Swish.* Through the hoop. Yeah!

It went in because Gianni really, really helped me by using his arms to help me throw it farther. Karina high-fived me and I didn't go low. I was too Holy Moly excited to get my prize. She hung a red, green and white Christmas bell necklace around my neck. I liked how the bells clinked. *Clink. Clink.* Tomorrow I would wear it to school!

"Hey, Gianni! Erika!" Justin was calling to us. In his hands he held black-and-white striped referee jerseys. "Put these on. We're going to start the game as soon as I tell Willa to stop playing."

"They look like a zebra," I said. I'd been to a zoo and seen cheetahs and zebras and all kinds of animals. "I don't know how to be a ref."

"I'll help you." Gianni took two jerseys and handed one to me. I took it and he put it over my head and helped me get my arms through. Then he put a whistle around my neck.

"Blow it when I tell you to, okay?" he said.

Suddenly, the big smile on his face disappeared and he was looking over my shoulder at something.

I turned. *Oh no. Oh no. Oh no.* The mean boys were back and were drinking ice drinks from the corner store. They weren't supposed to drink them in the gym. No Siree. That was bad. They were saying something to Bilal and he didn't look happy.

"Come on," I said, taking Gianni's arm. "Let's walk the other way. You told me that."

"Just wait, Erika. Bilal might need help. If he does, don't follow me."

Mr. Warner walked over to the boys and said something to them and they left with their drinks. Gianni let out a big sigh. *Whew.* I was glad they were gone. The band stopped playing and the gymnasium wasn't nearly as noisy anymore. But then a whistle sounded and I put my hands over my ears.

"Okay," said Willa in her microphone. "We're ready for Volleyball to take on Soccer!"

The volleyball team came running through the changing room door dressed in elf outfits and everyone cheered. Me too. They looked so funny. Their feet tinkled because they had bells on them. *Tinkle. Tinkle.*

Then the soccer team ran out dressed as reindeer! *Hahahahaha!* And they even wore antlers on their heads.

The game started and Gianni and I ran up and down and up and down. Running so much made my legs tired and I felt like I had rocks in my shoes.

Then Gianni stopped running so I stopped, and I was panting and panting. Gianni said to me, "Blow the whistle."

I put my whistle to my mouth and blew as loud as I could. Then I put my hands over my ears because it was loud. Everyone stopped running.

Gianni pulled a hand away from my ear and said, "Now say, 'Foul.' And point to Richard."

"Foul!" I pointed to Richard like Gianni told me to do. Everyone laughed. Then I laughed and laughed even though I don't know why I yelled "foul" at Richard.

Richard threw his arms in the air and made a big show of me yelling foul and I knew he was joking. The audience all started chanting, "Foul, foul." So, I did too.

The game ended and the soccer team won, which made me happy because Richard and Bilal, my new friends from *Grease*, had won. Justin wanted our referee jerseys back so I took mine off and gave it to him and the whistle too. Karina and Cameron came over to me.

"Great job!" said Karina. "That was fun. I'm going to suggest that the incoming Student Council make it an annual event."

"I got a basket," I said.

"You did," said Cameron. "I saw you sink it."

Karina fixed my collar like she always did. "I asked Gianni to drive you home because I'm going to Cameron's."

I wrapped my arms around her and she kissed the top of my head. Then she untangled us and said, "I'm proud of you."

"I called 'Foul.'"

She kissed my cheek. "That *was* funny. Now, go help clean up. That's your duty as a Best Buddy."

"Well, duh."

Karina shook her head but in a fun way. "I'll tell Mom you're going with Gianni and get her to hold your dinner."

"No," I said. "I can tell Mom myself. I'll use Gianni's phone. I want a phone for Christmas."

Karina shrugged. "Tell Mom not me."

Gloria and me and Madeline put all the basketballs away. One by one we put them all on the trolley. We did a good job. Willa and her singer friends took all her equipment through the same door as they brought it in. Marcie and Don and Mohammed took down signs. And Justin and Anna and Stuart and Gianni unfolded the prize tables and carried them to a back closet. I watched as Bilal and Richard carried a table together. They weren't Best Buddies but they were helping.

By the time everything was put away, the people and the noise were all gone.

"We should get going," said Gianni. "I need to get you home."

"I have to go to my locker," I said.

The halls were still busy with people who were also getting their coats and books from their lockers. As we walked, Gianni didn't talk very much and he kept looking up and down the halls and he didn't look happy like he did when he was in the gym being a referee. No Siree.

"Why are you sad?" I asked.

"I'm not sad. Just a little worried about Bilal. He needs a friend to walk out with."

"Those boys were bugging him n the gymnasium. That's not nice."

His phone buzzed and he took it out of his pocket, read his text message and then put the phone back in his pocket.

"Sonya said Bilal is okay," he said, running his hand through his hair. "He's getting a ride with Richard and a few of the guys on the soccer team."

We stopped at my locker and I turned my lock once around and then turned it the other way, then back again. When I had my door open I pulled out my coat and Gianni helped me put it on. Then I took my tam out.

"Do you like him?" I asked when I was putting on my hat.

"Who?"

"Bilal."

"He's my friend."

"Hey, Erika!" I heard Richard's voice. "You got me good tonight."

I put my hand to my mouth and giggled before I yelled, "Foul!"

He winked at me. "You definitely got me. I deserved it."

"Soon it's time to dance on the stage," I said. "I can't wait."

"Me neither." He patted Gianni's back. "Thanks to this guy here."

"I didn't do much," said Gianni. "You practised." Gianni looked around before he looked back at Richard. "Where's Bilal? Sonya said you were driving him."

"He's meeting me at the front doors. Don't worry there's a few of us."

I wanted to talk to Richard some more. "I know all the songs cuz I practised too," I said.

"You sure do," said Richard. He winked at me. "You're going to be a star in that last number."

"Come on," said Gianni, putting his hand on my back. "I have to get you home." He turned to Richard. "I'm glad you're driving him."

"That's the plan." Richard turned to me and winked. Then he gave me the thumbs up and walked away.

I shut my locker, then Gianni and I walked down the hall but now it was mostly empty. Outside, the parking lot was empty too as we walked out to Gianni's car. I tromped through the snow cuz he had parked it far away. *Tromp. Tromp.* I was pooped. And hungry. *Uh oh.* I forgot that I had to tell my mother to hold my dinner. "Can I have your phone?" I asked Gianni. "I need to text my mom."

"Sure," said Gianni.

He pulled it out of his pocket and handed it to me. "Why don't you send the text in the car? It's too snowy right now. You don't want to get the screen wet."

When I got my own phone, I would have to remember not to get the screen wet. "Can I put it in my pocket?" I asked. I wanted to have a phone in *my* pocket too.

"Sure. Just be careful with it."

"I know how to take care of a phone."

I carefully put the phone in my pocket. Then we kept walking to Gianni's car. The snow fell like little fluff balls from the sky. I stuck my tongue out to catch one.

Gianni started singing *Jingle Bells* out loud, so I did too. We sang loud as we walked to his car. I love *Jingle Bells*.

"Hey, Cipriano!" We were singing so loud we didn't hear anyone coming up behind us.

I turned to see who was calling Gianni. *Uh oh. Uh oh. Uh oh.* It was the mean boys. I counted and there were three of them and not four.

"Erika, get in the car," said Gianni.

"Look, it's Cipriano and his *retard*."

That wasn't a nice word and if someone called me that I was supposed to tell my mom or Karina if I was at school.

"That's not a nice word," I said. I didn't like how they had said that to Gianni. "And you need to show respect to my friend."

They all laughed and their laughing sounded horrible and evil, like a witch cackling only lower and meaner. One of the mean boys came up to me and stood in front of me. He had a space between his teeth, and blue eyes and blond hair, and a scar on his face like he'd been cut and it looked like a zipper. I knew I was supposed to walk away from them if they came near me, but I didn't have anywhere to walk because the school was far away. I could step back but I couldn't walk.

Before I could move at all, Gianni jumped in front of me.

"Don't go near her!" He sounded like he was growling. I'd never heard Gianni talk like that to anyone before.

My legs started to shake because something wasn't right. Gianni must have pressed his car door opener because I heard the beep-beep and click.

"Erika," he said in a low voice, "get in my car, okay?"

Another boy came up behind me and stole my tam right off my head. I put my hand on my hair. It was really gone. "My hat! That's my favourite hat!" I turned to see who had taken it and it was a boy with a spider tattoo on his neck. I didn't want him to have my hat. I wear it every day in the winter and winter isn't over yet. My bottom lip jutted out and a tear came out of my eye. It was *my* hat. Not his.

"You coward!" Gianni yelled. "Go pick on someone who can defend themselves. Give her hat back."

"All right gay-boy how 'bout we *pick on you*. How's that?"

"Boys can like boys," I said.

"Even the *retard* thinks you're a fag!"

The mean boy reached out to touch me and suddenly Gianni lunged at him and knocked him over.

NO! NO! I wanted to say NO out loud but I couldn't. It was stuck in my throat. The other boys swarmed in on Gianni and started kicking him.

"NO!" This time I yelled out loud. "Stop hurting him! He's my friend." My voice sounded so loud and high. My tummy started to hurt really badly and I wanted to cover my eyes. I didn't like what was happening. I had lost my hat and they were hurting Gianni.

"Get in the car, Erika!" Gianni screamed. "And lock it."

My hands were shaking but I opened the car door and got in. I had to do what Gianni said. I did. I pressed the lock button. Outside, Gianni was rolled into a ball but they kept kicking his back and stomach and head. I could hear crunching. *Crunch. Crunch.* It sounded awful. I didn't like it. NO! NO! Gianni groaned and held his stomach. Tears popped out of my eyes and rolled down my cheeks.

I looked down and put my hands in my lap and then I felt the phone in my pocket. I could call the police. I knew how to do that. Yes. I knew how to call the police. I knew what to do. I'd practised. My dad had showed me. When his hands worked he'd told me how to press the right numbers. He was the one who made me practise. I was supposed to call 9-1-1.

I pressed the number 9 then 1 then 1. A voice came on the phone.

"Hello," I said. "My name is Erika Wheeler and there's an *e-mer-gen-cy* at Sir Winston Churchill High School in the parking lot by the dumpster. You need to come cuz my Best Buddy, Gianni, is getting hurt." I wiped my nose with my sleeve. I could do this. My dad had taught me. I told the lady the address of the school cuz I knew it off by heart.

"Miss, is he hurt badly?"

I made myself look outside and I saw a boy pull out a knife and put it to Gianni's face.

"A mean boy has a knife. He's bleeding."

I sat low in my seat so no one would see me on the phone and try to take it away, like they took my hat.

"We'll send someone out as soon as possible," said the woman on the phone.

I quickly pressed the red button on the phone and held it in my lap. My body shook and shook and I wanted to go home. See my mommy and my daddy and Karina and Gracie my Build-a-Bear. The noise outside the car was still loud and I glanced outside and saw Gianni and there was blood on his face. I hate blood. He was curled in a ball and he was holding my hat like I hold Gracie when things were awful.

They were mean boys. I looked at the phone. I knew how to take photos. I did. Karina showed me with her phone.

Click. Click. Click. Click. I took one picture of each mean boy. I sat as low in the car as I could and I kept snapping. Gianni's phone rang but I didn't answer it because it was Gianni's phone so it wasn't my *personal business*. I kept taking photos. *Click. Click. Click. Click.*

"Hey!" I heard Richard's voice.

Suddenly, Richard was running over, really fast too. And Bilal too. And three other boys from the soccer team. Now there was so much screaming and yelling and I just couldn't stop crying because Gianni was on the ground, not moving, and I knew he was hurt.

"Let's get out of here!" The boy who had taken Harrison Henry's lunch grabbed his knife off the ground and the three boys ran away.

Gianni's phone rang again. But I didn't answer it. Bilal and Richard were leaning over Gianni, talking to him. I watched, hoping to see Gianni stand up and brush the snow off his pants. But he didn't. He just lay on the ground, curled up in a ball.

Bilal looked from Gianni to me. As soon as he saw me he

ran over to the car. I looked around and when I saw that the mean boys were really gone, I unlocked the door.

"Are you okay, Erika?" he asked, panting.

"The police are coming," I said.

"Did you phone them?"

I nodded.

"Smart girl."

"I took photos too."

"That's *brilliant*, Erika. We've got them this time!"

Bilal talked to me, and Richard talked to me too, but one of them always stayed by Gianni. But they didn't want me to get out of the car and see Gianni. I didn't want to get out of the car anyway. I didn't like blood. No! I didn't.

Soon I heard the wailing sirens. The sirens seemed to scream and scream. I hated how loud they were. The phone fell out my hands when I covered my ears. Blue and red lights flashed, and a police car raced into the parking lot and *screeched* to a halt. An ambulance followed.

The ambulance opened and a man dressed in a uniform came over to Gianni and talked in his ear. I wanted to see Gianni move. I thought I saw him nod. The ambulance people brought a stretcher and put Gianni on it. Were they taking him to the hospital? I didn't want him to go to the hospital. Hospitals smelled. I started to cry again. I wiped my nose with my sleeve.

The policeman talked to Richard. I saw him point to me. The policeman nodded and walked over to the car and opened my door.

"Miss," he said. His voice sounded nice so I stopped wiping my nose. "Are you the one who called the police?"

I nodded.

He knelt down to talk to me. "That was a smart thing to do."

"My dad taught me."

"Can I teach you something else?"

I nodded.

"Next time, if you can, stay on the line and keep talking to whoever you were talking to."

"It was a lady," I said. "She was nice."

"It's okay to keep talking to her. Sometimes that helps us. She tried to call you back." He smiled at me. "Now, can I talk to you about what happened here?"

"Yes," I said.

"I want you to tell me what you saw tonight."

I held up Gianni's phone. "I know what they look like and I took photos on my friend Gianni's phone."

CHAPTER FOURTEEN
GIANNI

E rika! I had to get her in the car. Now!

Then I saw an arm reach out to touch her.

No way!

My feet left the ground and I lunged at the guy. Hurled myself at him. We crashed to the frozen ground, the impact jolting me but ironically, also energizing me. No one was going to hurt Erika. No one.

We rolled on the ground, me on top, him on top, me on top. My size and strength gave me the upper hand for a time, and I pinned him with his face to the ground. I wound up to punch him and I almost did it. I totally had it in me to smash the back of his head.

Until I felt the boot to my back and a sharp pain seared through me. I flew forward, face first into the snow. Then the other two circled me and the kicking started, hard boots to my side and legs and arms and face. I tried to get up but was knocked down. When a kick landed under my chin, and snapped my head back, my survival instinct kicked in and I rolled into a ball and covered my head. Bruises on my body I could handle, but I knew enough about brain injuries to know it didn't take much.

Pain shot through me with each kick. A foot hit my side and I thought my body would split in two. This time the pain did not subside after the kick but stayed with me. More kicks hit my fingers, my knuckles, and another grazed my forehead.

What was happening with Erika?

I peered between my fingers and saw the top of her head in the car. Good. *Lock it. Lock it.* I tasted metal, blood. It trickled into my mouth. Erika hated blood. Then I felt the tip of something sharp.

A knife.

Voices sounded in the distance. My good Italian Catholic upbringing was revived and I prayed for help.

Voices. Oh God. Please. I heard Richard. Bilal's voice.

The noise around me escalated, shouting circled me like a whirling ride.

"Let's get out of here."

Cowards. Feet on snow. Voices yelling. And then the ringing started. Suddenly, a paramedic stood over me. "Erika," I muttered.

"She's okay."

"She needs her hat," I mumbled. They put me on a stretcher, hoisted me up, and put me in an ambulance. The doors shut and then it hit me. I'd been in a fight. Well, sort of. It was pretty one-sided.

The entire hospital scene was a bit of a crap show. I got wheeled in, put in a bed, and assessed for damage. Someone phoned my parents and they swooped in so quickly my dad must have floored it the whole way.

"We heard you protected Erika," Dad said while my mom fussed around my bed. He paused and clasped his hands together. "But, son, she protected you too. She's a clever little thing. Acts on her feet."

"Is she okay?" I asked.

"Erika's fine," said my mother. "Shaken up, but physically she's fine. She's the one who called the police."

"How?" I croaked. "She doesn't have a phone."

"She used yours," said my dad.

"Oh, right," I said. "She had it in her pocket."

"When the police came," said my mother, "she described those boys to the police officers, right down to the tattoos and marks on their bodies. Plus, she had photos."

"Photos?"

"She took pictures on your phone," said my dad. "Hopefully, they're all being charged with assault. And one of them could be charged with having a weapon. There could be more charges too. A young lady heard about it from somewhere—you kids and that social media stuff—and immediately phoned the police station, saying she'd also been attacked by this group too. Guess that crazy posting of too much information worked this time round."

"She had her hijab ripped right off her head," said my mother. "You're so lucky you weren't stabbed. I'm so grateful that those boys from your play came along when they did. And that nothing bad happened to Erika. She's such a sweet thing." She pressed her shaking hands to her forehead.

"Do you want Erika to come in here?" my father asked.

"She hates hospitals," I said. "She can see me at home, tomorrow. I want to leave now. Go home."

"Erika's in the lobby," said my mother. "She and her sister have been waiting to see you."

"She's waiting?"

"She wouldn't leave."

"Tell her to come in," I said. "If they'll let her."

When Erika poked her head around the blue curtain, the first thing she did was put her hand over her mouth.

"Do I look that ugly?" I asked, trying to smile even though my face felt stretched like rawhide over a drum. I hadn't looked in a mirror yet, and I wasn't sure I wanted to.

"Hi, Gianni," said Karina, trying to smile as well, but not doing a very good job. "Erika refused to leave."

"I'm glad," I said.

Karina took Erika's hand in hers and walked her over to my bedside. "How about if I leave you for a minute?" she said to her. "I'll wait for you."

Once Karina was gone, Erika said, "You don't look good."

"I'm alive," I said.

"I don't like those boys." She shook her head.

"I'm with you on that one," I said. "I heard you talked to the police."

"I told the police they should put them in jail." And just like that, the tears started.

"I'm okay." I tried to reassure her.

She kept shaking and shaking her head. "I said something that I wasn't supposed to say. Karina told me not to. She said it was your secret."

Oh no. "What did you say?" I asked.

"That the boys didn't like you cuz you liked boys and not girls."

Air got caught in my throat. I tried to swallow. It took me a moment before I asked, "You told the police that?"

She didn't lift her head.

"And Karina too?"

"I know it's not my *per-son-al* business." She almost stuttered and that meant she was really nervous and scared as well.

I closed my eyes. I wondered who else she'd told. Who else knew? This was definitely not how I'd wanted it to come out.

"Did you tell anyone else?" I asked carefully.

She lowered her head.

I exhaled. The names on the list of who knew were starting to pile up, but none of them included my parents. Unless, she had told them too. I looked at Erika with her head bowed.

"None of this is your fault," I said.

She didn't say anything back or look up.

"Erika, it's okay. You helped me because you called the police and the ambulance came and brought me here. I'm okay, you know."

She finally lifted her head. "I told them you liked boys and after that they kicked you even harder." Her lower lip jutted out and her eyes welled with tears, again. "I told the police that too."

I tried to sit up so I could see her better. "I heard you called 911. You saved me, Erika."

She stopped sniffling and wiped her face. "Richard and Bilal helped too. And the police. They have your phone."

"You were smart to call and take photos." I wondered how long they would have my phone.

"My dad tells me I'm smart too," she said.

"And you are. Don't ever forget that, okay?" I paused for a second before I asked, "Hey, are they out in the hallway too?"

"Who?"

"Richard and Bilal. I want to thank them."

She shook her head. "Sonya stayed with me, and Karina,

and Richard was here but he had to go home and Bilal never came to the hospital."

"Okay," I said and sank back into my pillows. Then it hit me. What if Erika had said something about Bilal and me? I closed my eyes.

She tilted her head and looked at me. "Are you still gonna be Eugene? Your mom said you could if the doctors said it was okay. Eugene dances with me. I want you to dance with me."

I wanted to scream but instead this absurd laughter bubbled out of me at the craziness of the situation. I chuckled out loud in the realization that not only had she told the police I was gay, she'd also told my parents I was Eugene. The movement in my chest from laughing made me moan in pain.

"Don't laugh," she said, "if it hurts."

Tonight Erika's honesty was creating chaos in my life. But, seriously, what difference did it make who I was in the school musical? That was a relatively little issue in comparison to the rest of my life.

I awoke the next morning in my own bed feeling worse than I had the night before, obviously the pain relievers were wearing off and now my body was just one massive bruise. My body ached, a dull throb that pulsed like a metronome. No broken bones though so my healing process would be that much quicker. I lay in bed and stared at the ceiling.

Erika had asked me about performing and I had no idea if that was going to be possible and, in all honesty, I would skip the whole show if it wasn't for her. The thought of dancing made me grimace.

But more than that, the thought of being in the spotlight in front of the student body made me want to vomit. What if they all knew about…everything?

I reached for my phone but then realized I didn't have it. Damn. It was my lifeline to text messages, emails, social media and news.

Slowly, I got out of bed. Every muscle in my body ached. I stared at myself in the mirror and groaned. I inhaled. I could make my way upstairs. I could. One step at a time I walked up the stairs and entered the kitchen.

"Holy crap," said Rob when he saw me.

"Yeah, I know."

He made a face, scrunching up his nose and moaning as if he was the one in pain. "That's a lot of black and blue, Bro."

"Thanks. I needed you to tell me that."

The twins flew into the kitchen but screeched to a halt as soon as they saw me. "Can you see out that eye?" Jerrod asked.

"I can *see* you're still annoying," I said. "Why aren't you at school?"

"The swelling will go down in time," said my mother. "You have healthy blood cells. That's what the doctors said." She paused before she looked at the twins. "I'm driving you. Get your backpacks."

"I never thought you'd be the one to get in a fight," said Jason. "I didn't even think you could throw a punch."

"I heard he didn't," said Jerrod.

"Zip it," I snapped. "Anyway, I almost got one in." I held out my hand. "How'd I get a swollen hand, huh?"

"I bet you hit the ground." Jerrod laughed.

"Leave it alone," said my father, waving his arms. He was dressed in his suit. "Your brother protected Erika like a, like a *man*." His accentuation of the word "man" rang funny. I stared at his face, trying to read whether or not he heard the rumour. As soon as he saw me looking at him he glanced away. Bingo. I had my answer. My heart thudded to the end of my toes.

"Why'd they pick on you?" Jerrod asked.

"'Cause we're Italian?" Jason asked.

Was it now or never? Again the lump, like a wet wad of newspaper, got lodged in my throat, like really, really stuck. What was wrong with me that I couldn't just come out and say what I needed to say?

I glanced at Rob and he made eye contact and raised his eyebrows at me as if to say *your call, Bro.*

This wasn't how I wanted it to be. I opened my mouth then closed it then opened it again. My family seemed to stand still like statues, no one saying a word. Or maybe time had just stopped.

I looked at each one of them. My mother ringing her hands. My father staring at the floor. The twins looking at me, waiting for an answer because they were Italian too. And Rob giving me the go ahead nod.

No, time never stood still.

After a few moments I sucked in a deep breath, exhaled then said, "Don't worry, they didn't target me because I'm Italian." Then I blurted out, "I'm gay."

There. I'd said it.

Awkward tension filled the room, and that pseudo-silence took over again. The refrigerator hummed, the wind howled outside, and everyone was breathing. Yes, I could hear them, and they weren't in harmony.

My dad spoke first. "I need to get to work," he said.

Nonna entered the room, wheeling her walker into the counter causing a bang loud enough to make everyone jump. "What's going on in here? I'm hungry."

"Gianni just told us he's gay," said Dad quietly. Then he grabbed his coat and headed outside. The back door slammed.

Nonna waved her hand in front of her face. "You young people. Always acting like everything is new. Huh. Zio Mario in the old country was a homosexual. Who cares? Not my business. Now, what's for breakfast?"

I spent the day in bed, mostly sleeping. Yup, the painkillers knocked me out. My mother brought me food but I wasn't hungry. I heard my father come home from work and dinner being served. And I waited. I waited for the knock on my bedroom door.

It came thirty minutes after dinner.

"Gianni," said my mother from the other side of my door. "Can we come in?"

"Sure," I said.

Both my mother and father slowly walked in my room. My mother, her hands clasped in front of her body, looked at me with her are-you-okay-head-tilt, and my father looked at the ceiling. Both looked like they'd rather be going to the dentist to get their teeth shaved.

"We wanted to talk to you for a few minutes," said my mother in this soft, concerned tone.

"Okay."

My dad stopped well before my bed, shoved his hands in his pockets and rocked back and forth on my feet. "Son," he started. "Your mother and I are fine with your, uh, your sexual orientation. I think that's the correct term?"

"Gay is fine, Dad." If he wasn't trying to be so serious I think I might have burst out laughing. But now wasn't the time. I could hurt his feelings. "Thanks," I said. "I appreciate that."

"Your mother and I love you no matter what," he said. "You know that, don't you?"

"I do." I could feel the tears forming behind my eyes.

"But, Gianni," he said seriously, "we're concerned about your safety."

My mother lowered her head into her hands and suddenly I saw her shoulders shaking and then I heard the sobs, her strangled breathing.

"Don't cry, Mom." Tears seeped out of my eyes.

"Last night was t-t-terrible. Just thinking someone could do this to you. You could have died, Gianni." She sat on the end of my bed and tenderly touched my face.

"Mom," I said, "if it wasn't me it would have been someone else. Those guys were out to get anyone different."

My father moved to my bed and touched my shoulder and I appreciated his gentleness too, a switch from his usual testosterone slap. Granted, I was injured, but I knew there was more to it.

"We want you to really think about where you're going to school after next year," he said.

"Uh, okay. What do you mean?" I have to admit this statement confused me a bit.

"The city and all," he seemed to be stumbling over his words. "I guess what I'm trying to say is..." he paused and swallowed then blew out air before he continued with, "I think there are places that are more accepting than others. We also think you might be safer in an arts program. You'll have friends."

If his comment wasn't so serious and honest I might have laughed or been angry but instead I had to hide a smile. "Dad, I'm not a leper," I said. "I can make friends no matter what program or school I'm in."

"You're right."

"We just want you safe," said my mother, touching my cheek.

"I know. And thank you again. You've made this so much easier."

My mother fussed with my covers for a few seconds before my dad blurted out, "Are you going to suck it up and be in that musical?" He flicked his fingers when he talked and his tone had changed back to Dad, and I was beyond ecstatic that he was acting like his over-bearing self again.

"There could be scouts, or whatever you call them there," he said.

"He's bruised! Can't you see that?" Mom gave my father a dirty look.

Okay, so now they were both back to normal and I liked this side of my parents a lot better.

"Hey, '*The show must go on*,' right?" My father puffed out his chest, and the peacock had returned to its perch, obviously proud that he had done well knowing that line.

"You're right," I said. "The show must go on."

"And that little Erika," said my dad. "She needs you even if you're not John Revolta or whatever his name is."

"Travolta, Dad." I paused for a second. "Oh, and that's another thing. I'm not actually him in the musical. I'm, like, his friend."

My mother shook her head at me. "Erika already told us. Why would you keep that from us?"

I shrugged. "I dunno."

"We are proud of you. Very proud. Don't ever forget that." She wagged her finger at me.

CHAPTER SEVENTEEN
ERIKA

"I'm glad Gianni didn't die," I said.

Karina and I were driving home and it was so dark outside, like someone had coloured the sky with a black crayon.

"Let's not even go there," said Karina. "That would have been awful."

"I would have cried," I said.

"Are you okay, Erika?" She looked at me out of the corner of her eye because she was driving. "I know you had to watch something awful."

In my mind I could still see Gianni on the ground, his face all bloody. Yuck. Gross.

"I don't like blood." I shook my head over and over.

"I know that. That's why I want to make sure *you're* okay."

"You did a good thing calling the police," said Karina.

"The siren was loud," I said. "I covered my ears when it left. I don't like hospitals."

"Yes, but they help people so it's good he's there."

"Will he have to stay a long time? Daddy didn't."

"He'll probably be able to go home tonight. He's just badly bruised."

"I want him to be Eugene," I said.

"Don't push him," said Karina. "If you know the dances, you can dance with anyone."

"I don't want to."

"I'm sure it will work out," said Karina.

We didn't talk for a few minutes and just drove down the road.

"I told his secret," I said quietly. "They kicked him harder when I said boys can like boys."

"It's okay, Erika. You were right. Boys can like boys. They were the ones who were wrong."

"I hate secrets. I hate secrets. I hate secrets." Now I didn't feel so good in my tummy. I had told Karina I was okay but I wasn't. I had an upset stomach and I thought I might throw up.

"Don't blame yourself. Those guys were out to get someone," said Karina. "It wasn't anything you said."

"I hate secrets," I said again, looking down at my hands.

"Gianni's secret is out now," said Karina. "So it's not really a secret anymore. Don't worry, okay?"

"Okay," I said quietly. Lots of kids had been talking about Gianni in the lobby at the hospital. I was sitting down and I heard them say he was gay. It wasn't a secret no more.

I glanced out the window at the empty street and the snow. "Gianni didn't die. I don't want Daddy to die," I said.

"Me neither," said Karina. She reached across the car and took my hand in hers. "I want to be as brave as you."

I stayed home from school for one whole day cuz I was sad

from watching something bad. But the following day, in the morning, my mom knocked on my door.

"Time to get up."

"No," I said.

"Erika, not this morning."

"No!"

"You have to go to school today."

"NOOO!"

My mom came in my room and sat on my bed. I pulled my covers over my mouth. "What if Gianni is back at school?" she asked. "I think he'd want to see you."

I thought about this. Then I pulled the covers down. "If I had a phone I could text him," I said.

"I've been thinking about that," said my mother. "I think you do deserve a phone. You've shown that you can use it appropriately."

I sat up. "I get a phone?"

"Yes. We will talk about it at dinner. Maybe you want to tell Sonya the good news."

"I'm going to school," I said.

I wore my favourite hat that Gianni had saved for me. When I got to school, Karina said, "Don't forget, you have rehearsal after school. I will come and pick you up at the drama room."

"When I get a phone I can text you."

"Yes, when you get your phone. Now, go to your locker."

When I got to my locker, Miss Saunders was waiting for me.

"Welcome back," she said. "I missed you yesterday."

"I get a phone," I said.

"That's awesome."

"Yeah, it's *awe-some*. I want to tell Gianni."

"I haven't seen him yet." She looked at her phone. "But we should get to class."

"I want Gianni to dance with me in *Grease* and I want to tell him about my phone."

"We have to go to class first, okay?"

"Whatever," I said.

I opened my locker and took out one book.

"You'll need your textbook too," said Miss Saunders.

Once I had all my books we walked to my first class.

"Yesterday, when you weren't here, everyone at school was talking about what happened," she said. "You did a good thing."

I looked up at her. "Did Gianni come to school?"

Miss Saunders shook her head. "He was away like you." She looked at her phone again. "We're late," she said.

School went slow like a turtle walking up a big hill and I didn't see Gianni. But I told everyone I was getting a phone. After school, Sonya met me at my locker but she wasn't with Gianni. I walked to the drama room with Sonya but it took me a long time and she kept trying to get me to hurry up but I didn't want to hurry up. I didn't want to dance with someone else at *re-hear-sal*.

"All right, everyone. Listen up," Miss Clark called out. "We have major work to do. We have one week before opening night. Today we are going to run through every dance."

Uh oh. Uh oh. Uh oh. Gianni wasn't there for me to dance with. My tummy started feeling sick. I didn't want to dance with someone else. No, I didn't.

"Tomorrow, we will have an acting rehearsal and just do scenes," said Mr. Warner. "I want everyone off book. No excuses."

Amanda put up her hand. "Um, are we ignoring the elephant in the room here? Am I the only one who is curious about who is playing Eugene?"

"That *is* a good question," said Miss Clark. "Mr. Warner and I are working on that one."

I didn't see an elephant in the room. But I did know Gianni wasn't in the room.

Suddenly the door opened, making a huge screech. *Screech. Screech.* I put my hand to my ears and turned, but when I saw Gianni I screamed and ran over to him, wrapping my arms around him. Then someone started clapping and then everyone else started clapping together and it was loud but like one big clapping sound.

"Not too hard a hug, Erika," he said. "I'm still a pretty sore."

"Okee-dokee," I said. "I'm getting a phone!"

"That's *awe-some*," he said.

Miss Clark held up her hand and clapping stopped. "I'm surprised to see you, Gianni," said Miss Clark. "You didn't have to come."

"I thought I'd watch."

"You're still looking nasty, bro," said Richard and he scrunched up his face.

"You have so many bruises," I said looking up at his face. "But your eye is open."

"By next week," said Gianni. "I'll be fine. Nothing a little makeup can't hide. The show must go on!"

This time everyone cheered instead of clapping and it got so loud I had to cover my ears. Again!

"Are you going to dance with me?" I asked.

"You bet," said Gianni.

"Yeah!" I put my arms in the air.

Miss Clark cupped her hands together and yelled, "Time is ticking! We need to dance, folks." She looked around the room. "Um, let's see. Bilal I want you to dance with Erika for her three songs, until Gianni is ready." She looked at me. "Are you okay with that, Erika?"

I thought about this. "Will Gianni still dance with me in the show?"

"I sure will," said Gianni.

"Okay," I said.

"Cue music!" Miss Clark yelled.

Gianni sat down on a chair and Bilal came over to stand by me. When the music started, I danced with Bilal and I didn't step on his toes. Not even once. No Siree. Not once. When it wasn't my turn to dance, I sat beside Gianni and watched. We did the songs twice! I was pooped. At the end of the rehearsal, I was tired from dancing so much and sweat dripped down my nose.

"Not bad," said Miss Clark after rehearsal was over for good. She turned to Gianni. "So, what do you think?"

He held up his thumb. "Looks awesome. I especially like the hip hop."

"Yeah, Erika!" Richard cheered.

Miss Clark laughed and held up her hands. "Okay. Okay. I love your energy and enthusiasm. Keep it going until next week. Now, listen up for a few notes."

The room became quiet again because when Miss Clark or Mr. Warner gave notes everyone had to zip it. That's what

Mr. Warner always said. *Zip it*. Miss Clark told us a few things that she wanted changed but I had a hard time listening. Then she said we had a *tech re-hear-sal* on Monday night and a *dress re-hear-sal* on Tuesday night. After Miss Clark was finished she said we were free to go. I immediately went over to see Gianni again. So did Sonya. But Bilal didn't. He talked to Amanda and it looked like he touched her like Cameron touched Karina. He liked girls not boys.

"What's *tech?*" I asked Gianni. "And *dress re-hear-sal?*"

"Tech is for lighting and stage direction. Long and boring," said Gianni. "But a dress rehearsal is fun because it's when we run through the whole musical, every song, every dance and we do it with music and costumes. But we don't have a real audience. We save that for opening night. Do you understand?"

"I'm gonna wear costumes!"

"You're going to be awesome." He paused. "No, let me change that. *We're* going to be awesome." He winked at me but it looked so funny because his eye was bruised and red.

"Yup. We're going to be *awe-some.*"

"I'm going to dance with you, girl," he said. "No matter what."

"Gianni is dancing with me," I said to my mom and Karina at the dinner table.

"That's good news," said my mother. Then she looked across the table at Karina.

"Tell her mom," said Karina.

"I want my phone." I frowned at them. I didn't like it

when they had secrets at dinner and made faces at each other.

My mom sat up tall. "Erika, it's not about your phone. I promise, we will get one this weekend. This is about Daddy. I'm not sure he is going to be able to come to your performance. He hasn't been well lately. I tried to take him out today and the cold weather is so hard on his lungs. He tires so quickly and the play is probably going to be over two hours long."

"I want him to come," I said.

"I know you do," said my mother, "but it might not be possible."

I crossed my arms, lowered my chin, and stuck out my bottom lip. This made me very grumpy. ALS made me grumpy. "I want him to come. I hate ALS. I hate it, I hate it, I hate it."

"I do too," said my mother in a quiet voice. She didn't shush me for saying I hated something three times.

"Me too," said Karina. She pushed her green beans around and around her plate but didn't put even one bean on her fork or any chicken or rice. *Swirl. Swirl.*

No one said anything for a few moments and I ate some of my chicken but it didn't taste very good because my tummy felt topsy-turvy.

Finally my mother said, "Enough. We can't and won't let ALS ruin your wonderful accomplishment, Erika. That's all there is to it. There will be a lot of other people coming. Did you know Jimmy and his mother are going to be there on opening night?" My mother cut her chicken and stuck some on her fork. "She phoned me and bought two tickets." She pointed to my food. "And your hip hop dance teacher is coming too."

I unstuck my grumpy face and uncrossed my arms. "Corey?"

"Yes, Corey. He asked me after your last class to bring him a ticket. Keep eating." My mom pointed to my plate. "You need protein to dance." Then she popped some food in her mouth.

"The whole school is talking about the show," said Karina. "Like, the *whole school*. It's getting more play than the basketball team gets."

"That's because I'm in it," I said.

Karina laughed and threw her napkin at me and I liked that we were laughing instead of being sad.

"Don't go getting a swelled head on us," she said, rolling her eyes.

"I don't want a swelled head!" I touched my head.

Karina laughed. "Forget I said that," she said.

"Don't ever forget, Erika," said my mother, "that your father is proud of you even if he might not be able to watch."

After dinner, I took my dishes to the sink. Then I went to the family room to see my father. He was sitting in his wheelchair, wearing his funny mask and staring at the television.

"Do you want me to read to you?" I asked.

"Please," he said.

I pulled my *Forever After* book out of my basket of books and plopped on the sofa beside him. I started reading and as I read, I looked at him to see if he was going to fall asleep. But he kept his eyes opened and listened. I kept reading but when I got to the end of the two pages that I usually read, I stopped. *Uh oh.* I'd never read further than this part out loud before.

"Keep going," he said.

I glanced down at the page and read four words but then I didn't know one of the words. *Uh oh.*

"Sound it out," he said.

"*Ex- hil-er-at-ed.*" I sounded each syllable.

"Put them together."

I did as my dad said and put them together and said "exhilarated" out loud.

"Good," he said. "Do you know what it means?"

I shook my head.

"Really happy."

"I like this word," I said. "I'm *ex-hil-er-at-ed* when I read to you."

He tried to smile. "Keep going."

So I did. I kept reading and every time I got to a word I didn't know, my father helped me. If he could still help me with my reading, why were all these other bad things happening to him? He reminded me of the snow. His mind was like the clean snow that glistened but his body was like the dirty snow piled up on the side of the road.

CHAPTER EIGHTEEN
GIANNI

To paint a picture that everything was all rosy about my coming out would be ludicrous and a big fat fib. When I walked into the drama room and everyone stood and clapped it gave me hope and a sense of false security that all would be okay.

My return to actual school was a little less exuberant and positive. I took the whole week off from classes and returned on Monday. Walking down the halls, I heard the odd snide remark and a few *faggot, flamer* and *fairy* comments. Sonya met me at the first hallway intersection and linked her arm in mine, and we walked together down the hall, strides matching, though mine were less buoyant than hers. She seemed to bob when she walked, her ponytail swishing back and forth.

"Glad you're back," she whispered. "I missed you. And I'm not the only one."

"Thanks." I kept my head down.

"Don't do that." She gently squeezed my arm.

"Do what?"

"You need to hold your head up and be proud of who you are."

"I just need to get through today."

"We have five minutes until the bell. Let's go see Erika.

She is so excited for this week and the show."

"We all are," I said. "I love show time." Walking down the hall with Sonya was better than walking by myself.

"Hey, Gianni," said a guy I played basketball with.

"Hey," I said back.

"Good on, ya," he said.

"See?" Sonya whispered, "Not so bad after all."

"You didn't hear the names earlier," I said. "It's so weird. I feel naked walking down the hall."

She grinned. "For the record, you've got pants on."

We rounded the corner and there was Bilal, leaning against the locker beside Amanda's, looking like a GQ model in a deodorant ad, hitting on the hot girl of his dreams. My breath caught in my chest, making it tighten. There wasn't a lot of distance between them, and Amanda was acting all coy and giddy and Bilal was responding, like he was really into her. Was it an act? Or had he been acting with me?

Sonya squeezed my arm. "Head up. Keep walking," she whispered.

But Amanda seemed to spin around just as we walked by them. "Gianni!" she exclaimed. "It's awesome to see you back."

"Thanks," I managed to say, trying to keep my voice steady. "I guess it's good to be back."

Bilal stuck out his hand and I reached out mine and shook it, and, yes, we looked like two guys meeting on a golf course. "Good you're back," he said, his words like blocks. "We need Eugene."

"I'm back," I said, faking a smile.

"We'd better hustle," said Sonya, saving me from any more awkwardness. "We want to see Erika."

As we walked away, Sonya leaned into me. "Never mind him," she said.

"Yeah, whatever," I said. "I'm good."

Erika was at her locker, head bowed in concentration, spinning her lock around, totally focused on getting each number right.

"Look who I found," sang Sonya in her perfect soprano voice.

Erika finished the last spin and unsnapped her lock before she turned. "Gianni! I have a phone!"

She pulled her phone out of her backpack and showed me. "I'm not s'posed to turn it on at school though." She talked faster than I'd ever heard her talk. "Only if I need it."

"It's very cool, Erika."

She tucked it back in a pocket. When the bell rang, Erika put her hands to her ears, something she did every morning.

After the bell was over and she had pulled her hands from her ears I said, "I'll see you at re-hear-sal."

"Can I eat lunch with you?" she asked.

"Of course," I said.

"I'll join you guys," said Sonya.

"Thanks," I said. I could use company.

I managed to make it through the day, and by the time the bell rang, the heckling and derogatory comments had subsided, as had the big "good on ya's," the thumbs up, the accolades, and the clapping. And I breathed a sigh of relief. Normalcy would suit me just fine.

Tech rehearsal went as expected. Stressful. Horrible. Nerves unravelling like a ball of wool rolling down a hill. Miss Clark could hardly keep it together. Mr. Warner freaked when Richard called for a line. And Andrew, our stage manager, lost it on more than one occasion.

Erika remained quiet.

"Are you okay?" I asked her when we were backstage and not on call. We were getting through the rehearsal at a snail's pace.

"Is *Grease* gonna be good?" She looked up at me with her eyebrows together and her mouth turned down.

"Yeah, it will be. Don't worry. Tech rehearsals are always a bit of a nightmare."

"Okay."

What was up with her? There was no *okee-dokee* happening. "Anything else bugging you?" I slung my arm around her.

She hung her head and her shoulders slumped so my radar kicked into high gear. "Talk to me."

"My dad can't come."

"Oh, no. I'm sorry, Erika."

"He won't see me."

A thought skittered across my brain. "You love watching videos with your dad, right?"

"Yup. We like *The Sound of Music* and *Grease*."

"I bet," I said cheerfully. "If we talk to someone in tech, I'm sure we can get the show videotaped. Then he could watch it at home with you."

Her face broke out into a smile and her eyes instantly lit up. "*Awe-some*," she said. "*Awe-some. Awe-some.*"

"I'll find someone to do it, someone who will do a decent job of it too." I racked my brains, thinking of who would be best, then I snapped my fingers. "My brother! Rob is great at videotaping events and editing. I will tell him to zoom in on you and I will give him the exact songs you're in!"

"'Alma Mater,' 'Shakin' at the High School Hop,' 'We Go Together.'" She held up three fingers.

"It will be an Erika video. Erika extraordinaire! Your dad can watch it over and over and you can even pause it when the camera is on you."

"Prom song!" Andrew bellowed.

"That's us," I said.

We waited in the wings until it was time for our entrance, and right on cue, Erika and I took our positions. The music played and we started the dance but after about twenty seconds Miss Clark yelled, "Stop!"

"Why do we have to stop?" Erika asked.

"They probably have to fix the lights," I said.

"I like dancing the whole song," she said.

"I do too. But today we have to make sure the lights are good and the sound is good. It's an important night. And we have to be patient."

"Okay," she said.

"You're being a trooper and a real pro. I'm proud of you."

"So's my dad."

"I bet he'll be proud when he sees the video."

The rest of the rehearsal was tedious and slow and I could see Erika's energy fading as the action stopped and started and stopped and started. Finally, we hit the last song.

"Tomorrow, this one will be fun," I said to her as we took

our positions on the stage and waited for lighting to set up. "I promise you."

"For this song I will put my poodle skirt back on."

"Cue music!"

The music blared through the speakers and Erika smiled from ear to ear when she heard the song. We moved to the music and her smile never left her face. When we hit the part where Miss Clark had added the hip hop moves, Erika did every move with gusto and total concentration.

Miss Clark clapped and made us stop.

"Erika and Gianni, on this one, I want you forward on that part of this number. Gianni, as Eugene, you make this happen. Move Erika up." Then she yelled back to the lighting crew. "I want them spotlighted for that hip hop portion."

I leaned into Erika. "You're going to be a star!"

When the rehearsal was finally over I could tell Erika was spent, as was I. Pain relievers and bruises and dancing were not exactly a great combination.

I eased myself into one of the auditorium seats and heaved a sigh. Erika was on one side and Sonya on the other.

"You okay?" Sonya whispered.

"I'll be fine."

"I can drive Erika home."

"I'll take her. I told Karina I would."

Miss Clark called for attention and immediately the room went quiet. We were down to the nitty-gritty now. The notes went on and on and I could feel Erika getting restless beside me, kicking her feet against her seat. I gently put my hand on her leg. "Stop," I said softly.

And she did. All in all, she had survived her first tech

rehearsal and that wasn't an easy feat for anyone.

Once we were given the okay to leave, Erika and I walked out with Richard, Sonya, and Claire. Bilal left with Amanda. He'd hardly spoken to me, and when he did he was perfunctory, polite, and passive. But he was definitely with Amanda on a romantic level.

"So, I heard you're going to testify," said Richard to me.

"Yeah," I mumbled. "I talked to the police and they said it would help their case. They also said I should file assault charges." I still didn't really want to think about how I was going to have to stand up in a courtroom, and say what had happened and why it had happened to me.

"You're doing the right thing," he said. "Those guys needed to be stopped."

I inhaled. "Thanks, Richard. I appreciate your support."

"My cousin is gay," he said.

It was funny how now that I was out, and in grand style I might add, so many people wanted to disclose to me how they knew someone who was gay. I guess I wasn't such a freak of nature after all.

"I hope they nail those idiots for a hate crime," said Richard. "That's what I heard they were going for. The one guy is eighteen so he could do real time. They don't deserve to be free. Sure they're kicked out of our school but that's not enough. I heard you're not the only one testifying, that they have others from different schools. When is the trial?"

Suddenly, my head started to ache. "I'm sure it's months away," I said. "The courts haven't nailed down any dates so nothing has been set yet."

Now that I wasn't afraid of parking my car in the school

lot anymore, Erika and I reached my car first and we said goodbye to Richard. I opened the door for her and she got in. Once I started the car, I turned up the radio because there was a song playing we both loved. We started singing at the top of our lungs. I have to admit, this was one of my favourite things to do with her, and it eased my mind, making me forget about my conversation with Richard and testifying in court.

Halfway to her place, Erika turned the radio down because a song was on that she didn't like as much.

"You want me to change the station?" I asked. "Or put on a CD? I've got the *Grease* soundtrack."

"What's *test-i-fy*?" she asked. She said the word in three syllables.

I stared ahead at the road for a few seconds, trying to think how to answer her, not wanting to get into it with her, but knowing she deserved some explanation. That night flooded back and I glanced at her out of the corner of my eye wondering how she was doing. She had been there too, after all.

"It means I have to get up in front of some people in court and say that the guys beat me up and why."

"Do you have to say you like boys?"

"Yes. I do."

"I want to *tes-ti-fy*."

She pulled a card out of her backpack. "The policeman gave me this and told me to call him anytime. I have a phone now so I can call him."

My heart beat with pride and I turned to look at this itty-bitty girl who was a loyal friend. "You're really something, you know? Promise me you'll talk to your mom before you make that phone call."

"I promise," she said. "Cuz I'm using my phone *prop-er-ly.*"

"Let's play the *Grease* CD. We have a dress rehearsal tomorrow night and you're gonna be rockin'. "

"I'm gonna *rock it.*"

We listened to the CD for the rest of the way to her place and sang at the top of our lungs, especially when the prom song came on.

When I pulled up in front of her house she asked, "Do you want to see my dad?"

"Um, sure, okay." I wondered how he was now. He must have deteriorated if he wasn't well enough to come watch Erika's performance.

Karina met us at the back door. "Hey Gianni," she said. "Thanks for bringing her home."

"His brother is gonna make a video of *Grease,*" said Erika. "I want to tell Daddy."

"That's a great idea," exclaimed Karina. "Why didn't I think of that?"

"Because Gianni did," said Erika.

Karina rolled her eyes. "Attitude."

Erika took off her jacket and we all walked into the living room. Mr. Wheeler looked thinner than the last time I saw him; his breathing was raspy and laboured.

"Hi, Mr. Wheeler," I said.

"Hi, Gianni." I could barely hear him speak.

"Hi, Daddy," said Erika. "Gianni's brother is going to make a video of the play so you can watch me dance again and again."

"Good idea," he said.

"You don't have your mask on," she said.

"I just took it off of him," said Karina. "I'm cleaning the hose. I'll go get it." She left and went into the kitchen.

"Excuse me," said Erika. "I have to use the washroom."

Once she was out of the room, I was alone with Mr. Wheeler. "It's good to see you," I said awkwardly. "Erika's right about the video. You will be able to watch it over and over."

"I want to...see her, live," he said.

Although his speaking was raspy and hoarse, I could still hear emotion and determination. Like father like daughter.

"I'll make sure my brother highlights Erika," I said.

"Thank you," he said. "I'm sorry...what happened to you."

"That's okay," I said. "I'm sorry Erika had to be a witness. But she she did a great thing, phoning the police."

"Smart girl."

"She is."

"Keep telling her. Please, for me."

"I will," I said softly. "I promise."

CHAPTER NINETEEN
ERIKA

HOLY MOLY was I excited! Opening night was finally *here*! Dress rehearsal was so much fun, like *soooo* much fun, but tonight my mom and Karina were coming and so were the Best Buddies and Jimmy and his mother and Corey. My costumes hung in a *garment* bag so they wouldn't get dirty. *Gar-ment*. I like that word. It's a fancy word for clothes. I wasn't supposed to eat with my costume on. No Siree! No food. No drinks. No nothing.

I carefully carried my garment bag over my arm as Sonya and I walked into the school. We needed to get hair and makeup done.

"Are you excited?" she asked.

"Yup. Holy Moly excited!" I had rumblings in my tummy and it felt like soda bubbles popping and popping. *Pop. Pop.* But I liked the popping cuz I love soda.

When we entered the girls' change room all the white lights around the mirrors were shining brightly and they looked like big stars. I clapped. They were so bright. I'd only seen those little round lights on TV. Gianni said I was going to be a star! Only stars sat in front of all those lights.

Miss Saunders saw me and waved. "Hey, Erika."

I walked over to her, holding my garment bag tightly in

my hands because I didn't want it to fall and get dirty. No Way José. I had to take extra special care of my costumes. Yup. I did.

"I have to help you get dressed before you do make-up and hair."

"I've got a shirt to wear over my costume so I don't get my costumes dirty," I said. "It's one of my dad's shirts."

"Smart thinking," said Miss Saunders. "Come on, let's find a spot for you to change."

There was so much noise in the girls' backstage change room because everyone was talking and warming up their voices and singing scales. Sonya sang *doe-ray-me-fa-sew-la-tea-doe* just like in *The Sound of Music*. Once I got dressed, I would warm up my voice too. I knew how because Gianni taught me.

Miss Saunders took me into a corner and I handed her my garment bag. "I can dress myself," I said.

"I'm here to help you. All the big stars have helpers, you know."

"I'm a star!"

The zipper made a loud noise when the garment bag opened. *Scriiiiiiiitch.* Miss Saunders pulled out my skirt and she grinned like the Cheshire cat in *Alice in Wonderland.* "What a cool skirt! Wow."

"Yellow is one of my favourite colours cuz I love the sun," I said.

"You're going to look amazing." She handed me the skirt. I put on my skirt, doing up the clasp at the side.

"I need my sweater," I said.

Miss Saunders handed me my sweater and she helped me do up the buttons. "I'm all dressed," I said.

Miss Saunders whistled. "Oh wow. It fits perfectly. You are so cute!" I put my arm up to my face and rubbed the sweater against my skin. It felt *soooo* soft.

"I need to put on socks and shoes," I said.

I sat down on a chair to put on my socks and shoes and Miss Saunders helped do up the laces. They were black and white and I kicked my feet a little as I looked down at them. *Kick. Kick.* Back and forth. They were what my mother called two-toned.

"Erika." A girl who was in grade twelve called me. She patted a chair. "Come and sit here. I'm doing your hair and makeup." She held up a leopard print cape. "You can wear this to keep your costume clean."

"I have a shirt," I said.

In my garment bag, on a hanger, I found my father's white shirt. When he worked, he used to wear white shirts every day. He would get dressed in his white shirt and suit and put on a tie, and sometimes, if I asked him to, he wore his Mickey Mouse tie from Disneyland. I lifted my arm up to my nose so I could smell the shirt because I knew it would smell like my dad.

"Go get your makeup done," said Miss Saunders.

"Okee-dokee."

I sat down in the chair and a girl stood behind me. I stared at myself in the mirror. Soon, I was going to dance on stage and be in a big school production and so many people were coming to watch and I was in my costume. The girl started fiddling with my hair.

"My name is Loretta," she said. She bent down so she was right behind me. "I'm going to make you look gorgeous."

"*Gor-geous*," I said. "I'm going to look *gor-geous*."

Using a comb, she swept my hair back and put some of it in an elastic band. Then she put all kinds of pins in it, which seemed to take a long time to get it just right. But I stayed still because my mother told me not to squirm.

"Hold your hands over your eyes," she finally said. "I need to spray it."

I did and she sprayed and sprayed and it smelt funny.

"Okay," she said. "You can open your eyes."

"*Pee-yoo*," I said. "That stinks."

Loretta laughed. "I'll agree with you there, girl."

She waved a red ribbon. "Finishing touch." Carefully, she wound it around my ponytail and made a big bow.

"You look like a real fifties chick."

"I look pretty."

"You look GORGEOUS." She winked at me in the mirror. "But wait till we do your makeup. Then you will look beautiful and gorgeous!" She patted my cheeks.

Then she put all kinds of stuff on my face and eyes too. I have small eyes because I was born with Down syndrome. My dad always tells me he likes my eyes. When I was little he would put sunglasses on my face and tell me he didn't want the sun to hurt my beautiful eyes because they were what made me *Erika*.

"Are you okay, Erika?" Loretta asked.

"My daddy can't come."

"Aww. I'm sorry to hear that."

She pulled out her phone. "I'll take a picture and you can show him what you look like."

"I want a picture with my phone too," I said and reached over to take it out of my bag.

"Sure," she said.

I pulled out the phone and touched the circle that had the camera in it. "Here is my phone and the camera."

"Great! Get ready…and smile!"

I smiled and she snapped a photo of me. Then she gave my phone back to me and I put it back in my bag. I'd put Gianni and Sonya and Karina's numbers in my phone. And Miss Saunders too. And Richard and Amanda and Claire because they were my friends. Loretta leaned down and looked at me in the mirror. "Hun, you're going to be a star!" She patted my back. "Now, go break a leg."

"I know what that means," I said. "To do your best."

"Right on. And everyone knows you will."

I slid off the chair and saw Sonya and she was already dressed with her hair in a ponytail and her poodle skirt on. Miss Saunders saw me and, with her finger, pointed for me to come over to her. My feet felt like they were feathers as I floated over to her. I wanted my feet to feel like feathers because that meant I was a real dancer.

"I want a photo of the two of you," she said. "Stand with Sonya."

Sonya and I stood together and Miss Saunders took four photos. Two with my dad's shirt on and two without. I looked at the photos and thought I looked so *gor-geous*. "Send them to me," I said.

"Of course."

"I'm going to warm up my voice," I said.

"Go for it," said Sonya.

I went through the exercise that Gianni had told me to do even though it tickled my throat. This was what real singers did to warm up. Yup. I was a real singer now.

I wondered if my mom and Karina were here yet. "Miss Clark said I wasn't supposed to look for people before the show."

As soon as we walked in the big room where all the cast was, Gianni saw us and came right over. He was wearing his funny black glasses and had his pants pulled up so high on his waist. I put my hand to my mouth and laughed. He looked *soooo* funny.

Miss Clark clapped her hands and the cast all gathered around her and Mr. Warner.

"It's show time, folks. You've worked hard, now let it go and have some fun out there."

Everyone cheered and I did too and I didn't hold my hands to my ears. My tummy swirled around but it was a good swirl like a milkshake in a blender.

One by one, Miss Clark called everyone up to give them a card. When it was my turn, I walked up in my dress, and it swished back and forth.

I took my card from Miss Clark and she smiled at me. "Erika, you make the world a better place," she said. "Your hip hop idea is going to steal the show."

When our meeting was over, we all put our cards in our bags. Then Andrew called out, "Two minutes!"

Miss Saunders came up to me and said, "I'll stay with you."

Sonya breathed in a big breath, like *soooo* big, and then she exhaled. Gianni jumped up and down, swinging his arms back and forth. I didn't know what to do. I didn't want to jump up and down in case I fell, so I stared at the stage. The stage workers had made it look like a big school gym for the first number.

"One minute!" Andrew yelled.

Backstage went black and I was okay with that because I had been through a dress rehearsal and Gianni had explained to me that the lights had to go out before the show began and sometimes we had to walk out in the dark. I didn't like the dark but today it made me feel happy. I was going to go on stage!

Then the lights came up and Miss Lynch, the teacher in *Grease*, started talking and her voice sounded all over the auditorium. I didn't put my hands to my ears. Gianni told me to try not to so I could hear when I was supposed to go on stage. I knew exactly when I was supposed to enter and where I was supposed to go. I listened just like I was supposed to.

Gianni went on the stage as Eugene and I could hear laughing. He said his lines and I waited and listened and listened. Then the lights faded and the music started.

"Go, Erika," whispered Andrew.

"Yeah, away you go," whispered Miss Saunders.

Just like magic, my feet moved me forward and onto the stage to stand beside Gianni. Then the lights came on. They shone so bright like the sun. I squinted to get used to the lights. Miss Clark told me not to look at the audience.

So I didn't.

Gianni took my hand and we started to dance. We had practised so much that my feet and hands and body just moved. I could feel my smile up by my ears. Eugene pulled me close and pushed me back, and then I flew under his legs and back up without flubbing. The music was coming up to my favourite part of the song. Now it was time to get in a line and do the hand jive and I did every move with everyone else, even when it sped up, and I only flubbed once.

The song ended and everyone clapped, really loud too, and it was time for me to go off. So I did.

I got backstage and I was panting like a dog. When I was on stage I didn't feel tired but now I was pooped. I wasn't on until the second half but I had to change into my prom dress. Miss Saunders took me back to the girls' change room.

"That was amazing! I watched you from backstage and you were fabulous."

"*Fab-u-lous,*" I said. Then I said it again. "*Fabulous.*"

After Miss Saunders helped me change into my red frilly prom costume, I sat quietly, waiting for intermission. But I didn't eat, even though my tummy growled. No Siree.

"If you put on your shirt, you could have some water," said Toni.

I put on the shirt and I smelled it again. He used to smell nice until he got sick.

She gave me some water through a straw. "Wearing your dad's shirt is the next best thing to him being here," she said.

I nodded.

Intermission came and everyone rushed to get changed but I didn't have to rush because I was already changed, so I sat still in my chair and waited for my next time to go on stage. I counted on my fingers how many more times I got to go on stage. Two more tonight. I held up two fingers. And three tomorrow. All my fingers and thumb on one hand were used up so that was five. And three more on Friday. I counted my fingers and it made eight. I would be sad when I had no more nights but I would be pooped. On Saturday, I would stay in my pajamas all day and watch videos with my dad and eat Honey Nut Cheerios without milk.

When the second half started I was ready to go on the stage again. This time I went on with Gianni, so Andrew didn't have to tell me and Miss Saunders didn't have to help me. We held hands as we skipped. Miss Clark had wanted us to skip. Gianni skipped with his knees almost hitting his chest and he swung my hand back and forth. I swung his back. I'd practised a lot to learn to skip. It's hard and sometimes my feet get tangled. My heart wasn't pounding anymore and all I wanted to do was smile because dancing on stage was so CHILL.

In the prom dance I swished my frilly red skirt back and forth because that is what Miss Clark told me to do. The bow in my hair was the same but still matched my dress, and my socks and shoes were the same.

Swish. Swish. Swish.

My feet slid across the floor and Gianni pulled me in and out. Then the lights lowered a little, and we were all supposed to waltz. Gianni and I knew how to waltz the best. I counted *one*-two-three, *one*-two-three.

Gianni made his steps bigger. He was trying to be a funny Eugene. I followed. His steps grew even bigger. Soon we were almost flying, we were waltzing so much. The audience clapped and Gianni whispered in my ear, "That's for us."

When the song ended, and the lights went out, I walked off the stage like I was supposed to and I didn't run. No Siree. No running in the dark. Miss Clark said not to run. Miss Saunders met me and she helped me change again, back into my poodle skirt and sweater.

Now, I only had to wait for one more song. I wore my dad's shirt and I sat on my chair and waited until it was my turn again. I didn't even kick my feet.

"Finale!" Andrew wore a headset and gave out lots of instructions.

"This is your big number," Miss Saunders whispered.

I got up and my legs were pooped from waltzing with such big steps. This was my favourite song. Sonya was dressed in her black outfit and looked *gorg-eous*. When it was my turn I walked on stage to get to my spot on time. Never were we supposed to be late. No Siree.

The music started and we danced. All of us were on stage dancing, so we couldn't take big steps. Gianni and I did every move right. Then…it was time for us to move forward. Together, we danced to the front of the stage and the big light shone on us. It was like the sun had the biggest smile ever. The music kept going and then it was time!

Holy Moly!

My feet pumped out the hip hop moves I had practised so much. My hands *rocked*. The audience broke out into huge cheers that were so loud I wanted to cover my ears but I didn't. No Way José! I had to keep hip hop dancing.

Finally, the song ended and Danny and Sandy said their last lines and the curtain fell down. We all rushed backstage to get in line for the curtain call. My heart skittered like a stone going over water. My dad had taught me how to skip stones.

Now I was allowed to look into the audience and see my mom and Karina. Miss Clark said I could look at the end.

When it was my turn, I ran out holding hands with Gianni.

Everyone cheered and stood up.

Except my dad!

He stayed sitting in his wheelchair! He had a bouquet of red roses in his lap. My heart beat so hard, like it was still hip hop dancing.

I let go of Gianni's hand and ran to the side where the stairs were. I didn't run down the stairs because I didn't want to fall but I walked as fast as I could. One step. One step. One step. Soon I was at the bottom. When I hit the bottom, I ran over to my father and hugged him.

"Daddy! You came!"

The audience cheered louder. My dad didn't speak or hug me back but I knew by the look in his eyes what he wanted to say. He wanted to say that he wouldn't have missed watching me in *Grease* for anything in the world. I had to hold my hands over my ears, the cheering was *soooo* loud!

Karina had tears running down her face and so did my mom.

"Happy tears," whispered Karina.

Mom pulled my hand from my ear and whispered, "Go back on stage and bow for us."

The audience was still clapping and whistling and cheering when I climbed the stairs back to the top of the stage. Now I was really pooped. Gianni stood over at the side and I walked over to him and he took my hand in his, squeezed it then lifted it up. Everyone cheered again. The rest of the cast came running out for their curtain call too. The audience stayed standing and when Sonya and Richard came out last I had to put my hands to my ears *again*.

We all lined up and I lifted my hands with everyone else and then we bowed.

The lights went out and it was time to go backstage.

Gianni kept hold of my hand until we were off the stage.

"Erika, I'm so proud of you."

"My dad came! He saw me dance."

"Go, get changed," said Gianni. "Put your costume away and get out there and see him. He has flowers for you."

Everyone talked excitedly backstage and I high-fived everyone at least twice, even Andrew and Mr. Warner.

"Take care of those costumes," yelled Miss Clark.

Miss Saunders helped me change and I was so excited to see my dad that she had to help me with my zipper.

"We're going to get you there." Miss Saunders was trying to help me hurry.

"He has flowers for me," I said.

Once I was in my own clothes, but I still had my makeup on, I went out to the lobby and the crowd was so big that I couldn't see my dad. The first person I saw was Jimmy and he held flowers in his hands too. He came over.

"These are for you." He handed me the flowers before he pushed his glasses up. Today he wore nice pants and a shirt with buttons. "My mom said we had to get you flowers."

I took them and smelled them. "Thanks," I said. "My dad came."

He pointed to the side of the room. "He's over there."

Jimmy walked with me over to see my dad. Karina took the flowers from my dad's lap and handed them to me. Now I had two bouquets.

"Congratulations, Erika. You were wonderful," said Karina. "That hip hop was so fun and you really rocked it."

"I *rocked* it," I said.

My mother laughed and hugged me and when she did

she started to cry. I pulled away and she smiled. "Happy tears again, honey."

"You were…wonderful," said my father.

Inside my body, my heart smiled the biggest smile it had ever smiled. Even bigger than Christmas morning when I got presents. I knew it did. I hugged my flowers to my chest.

"Here comes, Gianni," said Karina.

Dressed in his jeans and t-shirt, Gianni came over to us. "Hi, Mr. Wheeler," he said. "It's so great you could make it. Your daughter was incredible. And we still have a video for you to watch at home."

"Eugene is funny." Jimmy laughed as he said this to Gianni.

"I wouldn't…have missed it," said my dad.

Gianni pulled out his cell phone. "I want to get a Wheeler family photo," he said.

"I want one with my phone too!" I bent down and took my phone out of my backpack.

"I can take it," said Gianni.

I carefully handed him my phone. I was supposed to take good care of it.

I stood beside my dad's chair holding my flowers and my mother stood behind him and Karina stood on the other side.

When the flash went off I smiled the biggest smile I'd ever smiled. I did it. I sang and danced on stage. It was *so CHILL.*

And I was going to get to do it again tomorrow.

ACKNOWLEDGEMENTS

Thank you, thank you to everyone who helped with this book. Erika's character was created because so many people took the time to talk to me, read the manuscript, and give me advice.

I was blessed to have met Tanya, Rosalind and Michelle Ponich in Edmonton. Tanya, you are an amazing woman and I love you. Please, everyone, check out Tanya's website at www.liferewardsaction.ca.

Michelle, thanks for the sister info.

And Rosalind, (a mom), you were always willing to talk over coffee or in our condo elevator.

Sue Robins, I appreciated you inviting me to Aaron's fitness class, reading the manuscript, and giving amazing suggestions. Yes, the guns comment is his!

Monica Sawchyn, your first-hand knowledge of living with a teen girl born with Down syndrome made Erika. Thanks for reading and giving me teen lingo. I hope I did right by Tianna.

Steven and Denyse Newton, thank you! Steven, I love your Michael Jackson move. It made it to print.

Thank you to Erra Gauthier for her sister comments and to Bernice Greig for letting Hector be Hector.

Thanks to my mom for working at a home for intellectually disabled people when I was a teen. You taught me respect.

A big thank you to my nephew Ian Schultz for his insight

on Gianni. You are so kind and considerate and I think Gianni is too.

As for the many organizations I Googled, the books I read, and the lectures I attended, thanks to all the writers, speakers, and professionals.

And finally, a huge, huge thanks goes to Clockwise Press for working so incredibly hard to publish diverse books. Thank you, Christie and Solange.

Also available from Clockwise Press:
Fragile Bones: Harrison and Anna,
another **One-2-One** book
by Lorna Schultz Nicholson